The Calligraphers' Night

The Calligraphers' Night

Yasmine Ghata

Translated by Andrew Brown

ET REMOTISSIMA PROPE

Published by Hesperus Press Limited
4 Rickett Street, London SW6 1RU
www.hesperuspress.com

The Calligraphers' Night first published in French as *La Nuit des Calligraphes* in 2004
This translation first published by Hesperus Press Limited, 2006
This edition published 2007

La Nuit des Calligraphes © Librairie Arthème Fayard, 2004
This translation © Andrew Brown, 2006
Yasmine Ghata asserts her moral right to be identified as the author of this work under the Copyright, Designs and Patents Act 1988.

Designed and typeset by Fraser Muggeridge studio
Printed in Jordan by Jordan National Press

ISBN: 1-84391-430-1
ISBN13: 978-1-84391-430-3

Contents

To Fabrice

The Calligraphers' Night

I passed away on 26th April 1986, at the age of eighty-three. Istanbul was celebrating the Tulip Festival at Emirgan. My death was reported that very same morning by my son, Nedim, to the municipal authorities of Beylerbey, a coastal village that sits cross-legged like a tailor on the hills of the Asian shore of the Bosphorus. My departure was without fuss, like my life. At no time was I ever afraid of death, who is fierce only with those who fear her. No cries, no tears.

My death was as gentle as the tip of the reed dipping its fibres in the inkpot, swifter than the ink being drunk by the paper.

I took care not to leave any mess behind me; I tidied away my life and my calligraphic implements.

Qalams,[1] *makta*,[2] *divit*[3] and the whiff of ink they exhaled were within reach, standing in order of size and how often I used them, all at the same distance from each other so as to avoid any jealousy or quarrels. Once I was dead, they would have killed each other. So I departed serenely, abandoning my tools, tools that had become the extensions of my hand, the caresses of my fingers, faithful and obedient companions – having for a while been quite undisciplined, when illness and madness had overmastered me.

They were the witnesses of my death: they froze when death appeared, then breathed again when she left the room. My mortal remains were of no interest to them; they were quite content to take their leave of me.

I was buried the same day, as Islam requires, in the cemetery on Eyyub, a hill overlooking the Bosphorus, an inert piece of ground peopled with slender cypress trees. My stele was a gift from the University of Istanbul. It is in polished stone surmounted by a nice hat with a sculpted crown of flowers and fruit. The engraved plaque pays homage to my talents as a calligrapher and a pious woman.

There were six people gathered round my coffin: my son and his wife, the gentle, illiterate Murshide; Hateme, my younger sister; Muhsin Demironat, the director of the Academy of Fine Arts in Istanbul; and two of my pupils: Munever, called Muna for short, the most gifted; and the laziest one, Omer. Silent and serious, as if this event could not arouse any other feelings, they were more than anything relieved to see me resting in peace after the fits of madness that had continued to persecute me. It was all over with that damn trembling that had deprived me of the only gift life had presented me with – calligraphy, and its pretty little companion, illumination. Henceforth I was at peace, safe from all panic.

Once my body had been laid in the earth, Muna was the first to slip away, without raising her eyes from the ground she strode across.

The following day, my colleagues gave their pupils a swift overview of my oeuvre: in their view, I had reformed the traditional art of calligraphy by opening it up to contemporary variations, and had made the rules of the discipline less strict. Unusual remarks. Only Muna had grasped the meaning of my work and knew the secret behind my departure.

I departed during my sleep, absent-mindedly. And yet, on that particular day, I had felt in full possession of my reason, ready to confront my work in spite of the trembling that had seized my right hand, the only one that put up any resistance. Nothing has remained of that attempt, not even a single stroke or line. Resignedly, I lay down on my bed.

I had chosen my position with care, hesitating to leave my arms held out or folded on my breast. My hair was done in a chignon, low down on my neck, and I was wearing my teacher's suit, which covered my long legs. A recumbent effigy illumined by the light of early morning; my skin seemed finer and more transparent, with brown flecks here and there on my old hands. An eagle's profile like that of Sultan Mehmet II, an authoritarian chin; only my closed eyelids softened the traits of my face.

Never could I have imagined the tranquillity of that second. I was neither happy nor unhappy, just indifferent. And yet I had feared death. Petrified at the idea that it might spoil my mother's dead body, or lay hold of my son Nedim, born from my marriage with Ceri, a dentist from Anatolia.

I got to know Ceri after he returned from Germany, where he had studied. In spite of his Western good manners, he had remained as uncouth as the Armenian cutler who came braying under our windows.

Of that journey he kept the memory of the gloomy public baths and the women who were too thin for his taste. He wanted a local woman, young and with a traditional upbringing behind her; my virginity and my education guaranteed a prosperous hearth for him. Seduced by my sewing work, he paid hardly any attention to my first calligraphic compositions. Courteous in appearance, but inwardly crabby, he had chosen a profession in his own image: a dentist, someone who attacks the pain at its root. My future husband spoke little, like his patients as they left his surgery with numb jaws and few words. He was to yank out teeth, and the best years of my life, with the same brutality.

On the day we were officially introduced, I was so overwhelmed by the sight of him that I seemed intimidated. Ceri was no picture, with his stocky body, hairy eyebrows and bushy moustache. Nothing in his appearance pleased me, but this was of little importance in my eyes. He would always inspect the teeth of the person he was talking to – a habit that came from his job, he said, but one that made me feel ill at ease. His round eyes, staring like two big glass marbles, popped out of his head at the sight of my father's gold teeth, and scanned my mother's palate with widened pupils. When the patient was a person of importance, he would twist the slender point of his moustache in his fingers, impatient to lay siege to the other's jaw. My father took my silence for consent and fixed the date of the marriage. Not being very observant, Ceri concluded that I was not naturally inclined to effusiveness, and in any case he preferred the advantages of a generous dowry to any chatter. In my silence he saw submission, and in my obedience, admiration. My father placed at our disposal the modest *yali** situated at the bottom of the family dwelling. It had once been destined for the porters on our property, and now served as a store-room for furniture,

---

* Waterside mansion. [Tr.]

tools and fishing equipment. My mother transformed this in-salubrious shack and my father had an additional room built to house the dental surgery. In five years of marriage I learned silence and its daily tricks, pretending that I had not heard my husband's disagreeable remarks or reproaches, and acquiescing with a curt nod that over time became chronic. I progressively lost the power of speech, until the birth of our son Nedim: he came into the world to the accompaniment of a long scream that startled the seagulls lined up on the harbour wall of the Bosphorus. Ceri was surprised to discover that my voice could be so loud and shrill and deplored the fact that he was not the lucky man who had caused me to cry out.

This birth brought noise back under our roof, children's swing-cots created a semblance of harmony, and I realised the extent to which Ceri and I were totally different people.

My father was unaware of my distress: he took the same atti-tude towards the Soviet liners arriving from the Black Sea when they passed beneath our windows. Sympathy had no place at the family table. It was a feeling that had been proscribed ever since a *Mukkavit*[4] ancestor from the Blue Mosque had been sentenced to death and executed by Sultan Mehmet II. It was the task of this great-great-grandfather, may Allah have his soul, to call the faithful to prayer. His repeated lateness, caused by his siestas, had emptied one of the most prestigious mosques in the city. He made his case worse by presenting the Sultan with the calendar of auspicious and inauspicious days riddled with errors. Hanged for negligence. With the rope around his neck, he continued to recalculate the position of the stars in the astral sky of his sovereign. An edifying story: it taught us to keep the expression of our desires within reason and to submit them to the imperatives of existence. My father, who took the view that any marriage should follow the same criteria, found in the person of Ceri an ideal catch for his attacks of toothache.

I started to devote myself to exercises in calligraphy to console my hand for having been offered too hastily in marriage. Shifting letters about, making the lines deviate and stand out – this was *my* way of protesting against this marriage. But I always returned to a strict horizontality, as my letters were not sturdy enough to be torn apart just yet. So I set them back down on paper and outlined them twice as boldly. The name of the Prophet, declined in a circle around Allah, allowed zones that were sometimes dry and sometimes damp to glimmer through. The time it took to dry corresponded to the time one needed to wait for a visit from the Most High: no more than a minute in winter; a few seconds in the summer, with its heavy, stifling heat. Calligraphers never blow on the ink: accelerating this drying process is the same as expelling this divine presence. So I would slide the fleshy part of my index finger across the paper, a drop of flesh on the wet ink that grew smaller as one watched. Calligraphers have all tried to seize this divine presence, but none has ever succeeded.

We calligraphers know this ritual by heart.

The years went by, and from being a pupil I passed to being a teacher. Why hurry? Now that I am dead I no longer have to count the minutes. My memory is intact; memories are more tangible than reality. My life flashes past in front of me at the speed of light, assails me and then withdraws without warning. All that I could not grasp while still alive comes back to me intermittently. I am a witness to the visible and the invisible: now I can tell the whole story.

A jumble of memories; in the darkness everything is so mixed up. I am overwhelmed by these unruly reminiscences, unable to struggle. Why resist when times of happiness resurface? Especially the beginning of my career as a teacher at the Academy of Fine Arts; I was thirty, and that was also the number of students in the audience. I gave my first course in September, between the scorching heat of summer and the mild autumn days.

My pupils observed my precise, controlled movements. I dyed the paper. I covered it with a sticky preparation, soaked in a decoction of tea, then coated it with a protective layer to prevent the ink from penetrating into the fibres. Once the page was dry, I polished it with a flint stone; my pupils, fascinated, swayed to the rhythm of the stone on the now silky leaf of paper. With the help of threads stretched out at regular intervals, I traced a few lines, then abandoned my hand to the Prophet's tongue and to the *qalam* that drew the black, thick vertical strokes of a *hadith*[5]. I saw the ink settling down, anticipating orders. The distilled soot was well acquainted with this first introduction to calligraphy. But I enjoyed holding it back even though it was eager to stride across the page. It thought it could tug at my heartstrings by a black teardrop that sullied the page. I proceeded to inscribe; the point of the reed bent back out of sadness and drowned its sorrow in the inkpot. Its mission suddenly struck it as being intolerable. Certain *qalams*, it is said, crumple their tips, mutilate themselves until they bleed, so as to put an end to their careers as torturers. Impatient calligraphers cut them into a bezel shape and abandon them among the waste of the studio. A *qalam* that has been re-cut has a shorter life expectancy than a new *qalam*.

My pupils did not suspect the life that was contained within each of my tools, and contemplated the scene as if it were a still life. My instruments, servile to begin with, had accepted the most academic exercises: flowery interlacing spirals, margins illuminated in gold. Then they started to connive with my daring.

At that point I began to torture the letters, placing them in quarantine in the upper corner of the page, crowding them together until they started to suffocate. The words piled on top of one another, slew each other. A knowing and methodical massacre, a virtuoso combat. I was daring to do what my predecessors had never imagined.

One day I was seized by the desire to make the letters swell up to such a size that they would defy the laws of gravity. The name of Allah written in monumental letters glanced at me darkly, freezing me with fright. I would never have allowed myself these transgressions when I was a pupil in the Sultan's school of calligraphers.

When I had to do the traditional exercises, I would illuminate Korans, enlivening them with marginal rosettes, with *unwan*[6] and *cedvel*[7]. I excelled in illustrating prayer books to the praise of the Prophet, and I would draw on a double page the sanctuary in Mecca opposite the one in Medina. Two holy lands protected by one single brick wall. Then the tombs of the Prophet's companions with their cupolas painted in bright colours.

My master, the great Mustafa Osman, was amazed to see how enterprising I was and criticised my speed. He would spend whole days barricaded away in his studio, refusing all human contact, so as slowly to think through his last great work, the *tughra*[8] of the Sultan Abdülaziz.

It sometimes happened that one of my pupils would ask me the question that all the generations together would one day or another put to me: 'Did you find it difficult to make a name for yourself in this masculine career?' My answer never satisfied their curiosity; they were only ever half convinced. I would reply evasively, telling them about my perseverance, and the hard slog, year after year, of my apprenticeship, before I drew a first compliment (mingled with amazement) from my teacher. I had distinguished myself without ever attracting attention.

In those days, in the studio, I would pass unnoticed; I was the assistant of learned old men in whom dwelled the word of God. I would prepare the paper and ink, clean and tidy away the tools, make sure the studio functioned properly (and sometimes that it was clean). I looked after the comfort of these old relics of the Sublime Porte. Selim, the hundred-year-old calligrapher, could work only when he was stretched out on the divan, one leg folded back to ensure his stability. I had to prop up his back with cushions, rub the chill off his thin, bony leg, and massage his calf when a nagging pain shot through it. In addition, it was my job, depending on the season, to offer hot or cold drinks, to freshen up the fetid odour of their breath. Only Mehmet, the lame one, never drank – he had lost his thirst with his leg. His family had caught him swallowing the dry grounds of the morning coffee. He refused all assistance when he took his seat. So as not to humiliate him, I had been ordered to avoid his eyes until he had settled down. He had once been a great calligrapher, and suffered from his diminished silhouette; he could not tolerate the pity of others. He wanted an aura of authority and fear to surround him.

In short, I supervised the building that had been granted to these old men who had been shunted aside on the arrival of Atatürk, who had banished the Arabic alphabet, and calligraphy and calligraphers with it. The trembling of their hands became more noticeable from day to day. But they made it a point of honour to disguise their decline, and withdrew into solitude to escape indiscreet gazes. Nobody took it into his head to judge their work, but they talked about it at length among themselves and described in minute detail their imaginary master strokes. My studio was a refuge for dreamed-of virtuosities, a hospice for pretentious old men, and the antechamber of death.

At the end of each day, I would gather together their meagre productions, without so much as glancing at them, and proceed to their destruction.

As the only woman authorised to enter this pavilion, I had long had to put up with their ironic commentaries. They called me a camel because of my big drooping eyes, or a giraffe because of my long skinny legs. Mehmet deplored my lack of curves, and illustrated his remarks by tracing the silhouette of a *mim*[9], first fat and then thin. The undulation of the letter was as essential as a woman's large backside or generously proportioned bosom – so his neighbour would hiss at me, sketching an obscene graffiti on the wall. Only Selim spared me. He continued to paint; his hand remained sure and had gained in skill. It was enough to make you believe that his sickly legs had yielded their strength to his right hand. He would work in absolute silence, far from the chatter of his colleagues, and claimed to write under the close scrutiny of the Prophet. He was the only one who prayed five times a day, and he found it difficult to prostrate himself; I also had to help him to perform his ablutions. Compared to his fellows, he was the least crazy, the most adroit and the most pious. I can still hear the murmurs slipping down his glittering beard, declaiming the *hadith*, and the noise of his fingers as they gathered each of the syllables he uttered. The precise marriage of word and wrist guaranteed the oneness of God. He would call me to witness his sermons, urging me never to depart from the paths of virtue and to follow the light of the Most High. The breath of his aphorisms swept across my face. His faith had the same smell as the coarse, soapy linen of his tunic; his piety breathed out the odour of the martyrs.

His colleagues would like to have seen him rotting away in a home; they called him a false prophet. Their slanders left him as impassive as marble. His black gaze accused them of wandering from the straight and narrow. He viewed them as offspring of the camel. In vain I would try to calm the most persistent of them and beg them to get on with their work. They forgot Selim and returned to their illusionists' exercises. Old Ali would show me his pages, still pure and white, and launch into an incoherent and verbose monologue to explain to me the meaning of the nonexistent lines and the techniques that had produced his absent ornamentation. I enthusiastically admired this exercise in pure, empty vacancy. My kindness made him voluble; he would vaunt his own gifts (unweakened by age), then make me swear not to divulge their secret to his comrades – they were all thieves, all too capable of pillaging his ideas.

I was obsessed by the desire to flee from this studio. But one of the men had only to put the least little drawing in front of me and, disarmed, I would cease to think about leaving this desolate place, the last refuge of apprentice calligraphers. The youngsters would arrive, stroll through the rooms, and leave looking sorrowful. The rising generation would sweep away these meticulous writings and mysterious apparitions. Technicians were about to replace my magicians. My melancholy sorcerers stopped copying the murmurs of Allah, who could hardly feel welcome in the new premises. Little by little he deserted these places in which prayers and incantations were no longer heard, forced to give way to the popular and patriotic slogans of the Grey Wolf of Ankara.[10]

Lined up on my bookshelves, the little sculptures with their dervish effigies were in a state of exaltation. Heads bowed, arms folded on their chests as a sign of submission, they were borne along by the incantations from the neighbouring minaret. I could not hold back a tear at this sight. Freed from their chalk, these figurines stirred at the sound of the song. Their tapering headgear enfolded the air in a repeated embrace, drawing perfect circles. I let them get on with it: their freedom was short-lived; they would soon resume their hieratic poses. Sometimes I could just make out a smile or a slight loss of balance, which made their prominent calves wobble, but they immediately pulled themselves together, obeying the cruel laws of inertia. Getting caught up in the game, my *qalam* followed their circumvolutions. Paper was not necessary, neither was ink. My wrist was too rigid to grasp their whirlwind movements. The stem of the reed rubbed its belly against the blotting paper, and turned round on itself. The groove in the tip became invisible to the naked eye, and was slowed down by the ink with which it was loaded. The tip set itself down obliquely on the paper and the trance continued. The opaque black colour submitted to the enchaining of letters, in a shapeless script. Before my dazzled eyes, the phrase inscribed on the dervish's headgear spread out: 'Oh our sweet Jalal al Din Rumi'.[11]

This is how I killed time. Dusting the knick-knacks in the house was a good excuse for avoiding Ceri's company. I would hurry away from him, pricking up my ears for the creaking on the parquet floor so that I would not have to bump into him. I was able to recognise his footsteps, his throaty cough after meals and his garglings in the evening before he went to sleep. I was forever putting off the time when I would have to go and join him in bed. At his first snore I would slip into bed beside him, reassured by the resonant proof that he had fallen into a heavy sleep.

Fearing that my dentist of a husband might transform them into false teeth, my alabaster dervishes played dead whenever he was around. The quack from the Asian shore of the Bosphorus knew the secret of teeth better than anyone and could whip them out quite painlessly. Then they were classified, arranged in order of size and in accordance with their distinguishing features. Ceri cherished them so fondly that he could now, at a glance, guess what was wrong with them, which way they had grown, and their exact relation with the gum. The human race was of no interest to him, not even his wife – too healthy for him, difficult to manipulate and to fit into his classifications.

We were both obsessed with cleaning and tidying; his office was polished every day, his tools disinfected after each use, and his drills, barbed broaches, electric polishers and abrasives vied in cleanness with my calligraphic equipment. Caresses and displays of affection were replaced by this hysterical hygiene. Our son, Nedim, had a bit of peace and quiet between seven and eight in the evening, when we proceeded to perform this daily ritual, he in his dental surgery and I in my cramped little shack that had been transformed into a studio.

I thought his profession was a sinister one. Didn't it consist in treating the only visible part of the skeleton? The part that was left after life? A gaping jaw allowed me to guess at the bony profile of a fleshless, mocking skull. I started to loathe the howls of his patients, the sound of the drill digging into the oxidised teeth. The sight of children lucky enough to have immaculate molars, clamping their mouths tight shut when Ceri asked them to open wide, filled me with joy. In order to amuse them, he would tell them stories about caves and grottoes, and explorers venturing into the depths of the earth, that vast decaying mouth.

As Ceri's treasury of teeth grew day by day, his cabinet ended up resembling the catacombs.

On one occasion, as old Selim was staring at the sky in search of inspiration, I was able to my great surprise to discover that he had lost his teeth, all apart from one, enthroned like a turban on his lower gum. He explained to me with a knowledgeable air that this one guaranteed the balance of his calligraphic compositions, as his tongue could rest on it while he was working. The precision of his hand depended on the solid anchorage of this molar that had become his collaborator. Planted there like a stele, it was his only friend. No way of taking him along to my dentist of a husband; Selim feared his fierce wild eye and his pincers ready to pull. The poorer and more underprivileged the patient, the more enthralling the dentist's examination became. Ceri was convinced that well-off people were of no interest to the science of oral disease. Since they did not look after themselves, the poor deteriorated more quickly.

Old Selim hanged himself one morning with his green turban, the one he usually wrapped around his fez. He had thought up an infallible way to do it, using the iron bar on the window. Nothing in his face gave any indication of strangulation. He looked no different from other days, perhaps a little taller with his bare feet touching the chalky ground. The damp traces of his two toes sketched the beginnings of an indecipherable piece of writing, the secret of which he had taken with him. I can still hear the echo of his words, murmured with what little breath he still had. Words I had to guess at across the porous partition of the wall on which he leant.

For the first time, I looked at a dead man with composure. In my eyes, Selim had been dead for a long time. It was strange, observing his corpse. He would no longer greet me, nor would he thank me when I brought him his equipment. His fingers would never again wolf down the midday meal. Old Selim would no longer insult his companions or speak ill of them. Relieved of his routine tasks, he would leave his great weariness behind him. The work he had produced, dazzling at the start of his career, had become peopled with unsettling silhouettes, composite beings from elsewhere, from beyond the inhabited world; the volutes of his foliated scrolls had metamorphosed into arachnidan traps, zoomorphic creatures, hybrid fauns. This bestiary that rose from his hands terrified him, besieged his slumbers, and seeped into every mouthful of bread.

He owed this malady to malevolent characters to whom he gave the names 'Gog' and 'Magog'. They had come to announce his imminent death. His words seemed to suggest that he alone was able to stop them drinking up the water from the rivers and prevent them gaining access to the cisterns. He would slow down as he spoke, and then, with a voice from beyond the grave, he complained that he had been abandoned by his only light, our Prophet.

Selim grew irritable when his hand refused to obey him. In vain he tried to draw it towards a universe peopled with *dîw*[12] and *djinns*,[13] towards decorative illusions that pulled him ever further from the Creator instead of bringing him closer. He took this as a rejection, and retreated into a disquieting silence, rebuffing all human contact.

He was able to turn into an inert surface, so when I saw his corpse, the idea that he was making fun of us crossed my mind for an instant. But I could see no spark in his eyes, no furrowing of his brows. The dangling palms of his hands were deserted by the happiness granted to believers. People came and slipped him out of the scarf that had strangled him; he was as stiff as his *qalams*, as hard as the wood of his paintbrushes. The two men who laid him in earth recited the only sura they knew by heart, thus ensuring that a semblance of ceremony accompanied his burial. No doubt Selim's soul would wander for years on end within the walls of our school, looking for his calligraphic equipment, his sheets of pure white cardboard, his *makas*[14] given him by Zühdi Efendi, the calligrapher of the great Sultan Abdülmecid. His desk blotter dotted with anecdotal signatures and his eviscerated oriental slippers would no longer afford him their comfort.

To my great surprise, when I started to tidy away his things, I found a parcel addressed to me. Under the piece of string that tied the whole package together there was inserted a slip of paper with my name, 'To Rikkat', carefully written. A precious gift, a proof of the affection he bore me, his way of thanking me for having helped him and so often obeyed him.

Crossing the Bosphorus with my booty seemed to take forever. Standing on the forward deck, I gazed impatiently in the direction of Beylerbey, longing to step onto the ground of its landing stage. My husband's rotating drills would be my accomplices; I would now be able to tidy my studio in all tranquillity and make it worthy of the treasure that would change my life.

I set out the documents in order of size and opened the Koran, signed on the colophon, given to Selim by his master; then I proceeded to the ritual gestures once performed by Selim, who paid it reverence every morning by planting a devout kiss on it. Over time, this ceremony became my own. I imitated the dead man, became one with him, opened the case of dark red velvet in which he had kept his *makas* and *divit*, index finger and thumb coiled in the silver rings. His last will and testament had bequeathed them to me. Selim must have explained to them the cause of his precipitate departure and his desire to place them in the hands of a person in whom he could trust.

My new companions took their place on my work table next to my apprentice equipment, which now seemed drab in comparison. I carried on with my explorations, my mind quietened by the thought that I had set them out correctly, and promised myself I would never separate them, never leave them. They became an integral part of my body, an extension of my hands, the accomplices of my calligraphic escapades. An oval tube contained Selim's treasure, an ink obtained from leaves that had been pulverised and then diluted in a honey-based solution. I guessed at the long hours of preparation this had required. I saw Selim filtering and re-filtering the juice thus produced: an activity that could always be improved, doubtless giving him a vision of the soul escaping from matter. A sort of ecstasy would overwhelm him as the gold shed its impurities. In all my life as a calligrapher, I never held such a pure liquid in my hands. The question of how to use it, and the quality of the paper that would be able to receive it, soon arose.

Selim's soul was scrutinising my fingers, watching over my reactions with tenderness, examining how I would welcome his tools. I was his only heir, and I needed to show myself worthy.

Thus it was that I became a calligrapher. This legacy, capable of transmitting to me the talent of a virtuoso calligrapher, would long preserve its master's habits, the skill of his hands and the agility of his fingers. Aware that this heritage was to turn my life upside down, I kept it secret, I hid my joy just as I had become accustomed to hide my pain, and just as easily. We calligraphers are impenetrable; ink teaches us to remain opaque.

I rummaged around in his papers and to my great stupefaction discovered some personal documents: old letters from another century, another humankind; photographs; fragments of calligraphy illustrating poems and *hadith*; and the *firman* of a rolled-up official text, on which the grains of sand scattered by an impatient sponsor were still visible. This expedition into his private life showed me a new face of my master – unrecognisable, almost youthful. The expedition came to an end when I came across a letter that was as enigmatic as the oracles of antiquity. I could spend the rest of my life deciphering this message in an attempt to understand the reasons for Selim's suicide.

I am the marabout of God. My inkpot has endlessly sung his glorious victories. His throne has never ceased to illumine my paper, my grave. His religious and military injunctions have laid siege to my sheets of cardboard like a garrison of soldiers with alphabetic silhouettes. The suppleness of my letters assured the general that these conquests were certain.

I saw the façade, the vault and the pediment of his envoy and I devoted years of reconstruction to it, but the inhabitants of his palace made me forget his sovereign expression.

Those eyebrows, two unsheathed swords, and his moonshaped forehead have shot icy, accusing glances at me. His lips have made the marbled paper waver. His breath, like that

of a desert nomad, has filled my studio with its fragrance,
drenched my paper with the bitter odour of his sanctity. His
punitive decrees and his archaic wrath terrorised my tools
that reproached themselves for such audacity.

There came a day when his breath ceased to irrigate my
ink, and my hand fainted when he left me. I have often called
out to him, but he has never deigned to reply. Then I decided
to join him in his dwelling to implore him to forgive me.

I am still waiting to be granted a hearing.

How long did Selim wait for his hearing, and was he pardoned?
Nobody knows. I myself would undergo the same punishment
years later, when calligraphers, approaching death, succumb to
madness.

This calligraphic farewell gave me a glimpse of his torment
when he said he had been abandoned by his only light: the
Prophet.

I shut myself away in the secret of my master, refusing to share it
with anyone. The idea of lending ordinary words to this narrative would have deprived it of all its magic.

I forgot Selim so that he might find repose, I forgot his enigmatic farewell and his malicious gossip and I settled down to
work. The idea of handling his equipment, impregnated as it
was by his blasphemies, terrified me. *Qalams* and paintbrushes
showed no enthusiasm for the task. In any case, I must not seem
to be asking them to show their talent – I kept my admiration or
my exhortations quiet, and they preferred to display themselves
little by little, as and when they wished. They came to me, play-
fully, helped me to refine my compositions before putting their
mourning dress back on. They vibrated between my fingers,
borne along by those stolen moments, before getting a grip on
themselves, ashamed at having tasted happiness. In time, we

were tamed. Our work gave off a whiff of pleasure and sin. Every kiss gave birth to a line, every embrace to a page. Selim's tools lay on the page. The *qalam* was forever demanding the inexhaustible reservoir of ink. The black streaks resembled nothing, my hand allowed itself to be guided in different directions. And yet, the thought was precise. Once the sketch was complete, I needed a brief moment to understand its meaning. Sitting at my desk, I was unwittingly drawing my own portrait, as seen by an unseen Selim. I realised that he had opted for the little stool placed under the window of my studio, already imbued with the odour of his ink and his old sweat. His visit marked the start of our first collaboration. The opportunity came up again a year later, the day when the *medersa*[15] decided to announce a competition with the aim of bringing forward anonymous practitioners of the art of calligraphy, capable of giving new life to the discipline. Out of one hundred candidates, they chose one woman: Rikkat Kunt, the daughter of Nessib bey of Beylerbey, the wife of Ceri Ince, the only dentist on the Asian shore of the Bosphorus.

I impose a strict discipline on my pupils. Their curiosity about me is insatiable. And yet we have better things to do; their hands are still clumsy and their writing wounds the paper. Their eyes do not yet have the intuition of the enlightened calligrapher. I allude to my career without touching on my life.

Propped on their seats, they settle down to listen to me. Muna asks me to tell them about the competition of 1936, a milestone for a whole generation of calligraphers. They offer me their bated breath in the same way as one proffers an inkpot. Ascending and descending curves and long loops give life to my narrative, and sounds come thronging to my lips. My audience drinks in my words, and tries to reconstitute the scenes. As a result, the same personage can inspire a host of clones that takes over their imaginations. Fifty years separate us from these memories, and when I speak of them, it seems to me that I know this history as well as I know the back of my hand.

In 1928, the Turkish Republic replaced Arabic script by a modified version of the Latin alphabet. The new alphabet was presented to Mustafa Kemal on a tablet of gold. The long genealogies of the different calligraphers, the legends related about them, as well as their unflattering nicknames, 'the poor', 'the hunchback', or 'the fisher', vanished for good, as did the exact location of their forever anonymous tombs. Religious grievances ceased to provide a subject for compositions. The spiritualism of 'fine handwriting' was no longer in vogue.

In 1936, the offices of instruction in the arts of writing were transferred to the Academy of Fine Arts in Istanbul where I taught. The reform had considerably impoverished the profession, both through the disappearance of illustrious artists and through the failure to transmit a skill that was doomed to fade into oblivion. Another problem that arose was that of the conditions of conservation of those works that future generations would need to ensure.

Did my voice reach the ears of old Selim, who had become facetious since his death? He amused himself by hanging around in my classes; the Beyond definitely had not lived up to his expectations. I was never hostile to his presence, with the exception of one morning, when he caused a considerable disturbance in my studio. In memory of this incident, I ceased to mention his name, his work, and even the way his life had ended, however characteristic it was of this historical transition.

The competition was devised to discover young talents and confirm that Turkey was well prepared to foster this discipline. There were a hundred of us candidates from different regions of the country: from the Black Sea, Anatolia, and, of course, Istanbul. Most of us had our own equipment. The most impoverished counted on the generosity of the organisers to provide them with a minimum of accessories. Others ostentatiously set out their equipment on their desks. I had laid out Selim's tools, and that fine old gold ink of his, preciously preserved for years. I took care not to attract any envious glances, and settled down in readiness for a whole day's work. My neighbour helped me to prop up the leg of my desk and introduced himself to me. Necmeddin Okyay would become my friend.

My pupils ask me for more details about the man who has become, in all of their eyes, an emblematic figure of the profession. Without going into it too deeply, I mention his gift for archery, his unequalled talent in illumination and marbled paper. Later on, he was appointed as imam at the Yeni Djami Mosque, but I am much less well acquainted with his talents as a theologian than as a calligrapher.

On this competition our future depended. A climate of meditative silence hovered over the hall. We had all been given the reproduction of a *levha*[16]. The test involved copying it with the highest possible degree of precision, imitating to perfection the medallion inscribed with a *bismillah*[17] and a verse from the Koran set out in mirror form, so that it could be superimposed on itself right way up and upside down. The writing was in gold on a black background. The candidates from modest homes were given a vulgar yellow paint. The others benefited from the generosity of their families. I was enriched by the last breath of Selim, condensed in the liquid, and by his skill, which even in death did not fail.

That day his accessories came back to life, and I had to struggle like mad to hold back their need to make up for the wasted years. An improvised concerto played itself out before my eyes: the *qalam* was a flute in my fingers, its support tried out its skills as an archer, and the paper became a musical score for the needs of all.

They scrupulously obeyed Selim's directions as he supervised their comings and goings and the erotic figures they traced on the cardboard-backed paper. The dead man did his utmost to remind them that pleasure owed nothing to the model imposed; their copulation with the paper should not stiffen into a divine obeisance, but rather engender an obscene tangle of letters. The instruments drew new inspiration from this, separated out from one another and then returned to the page so as to reproduce the initial figure. Selim himself could no longer distinguish between copy and model. The illusion was maintained even in the reflections of ink. The stiffening letters continued to exchange sighs of contentment through the golden liquid.

Had I contributed to this work? I still wonder. Perhaps the letters had left Selim's pious hands to land in mine, avid for new experiences.

At the end of the day's session, the candidates tidied away their equipment and left their pieces to dry under the close surveillance of the teachers who walked up and down in the hall looking for the perfect work. They discussed the ones that were rivals for the prize, and argued in favour of this one or that. This inaudible conferring filled us with trepidation. I preferred to await the official announcement of the results that would be made by Ismail Hakki, the director of the *medersa* for calligraphers.

My family had been surprised to learn of my ambitions. Ceri was even more amazed to see me taking part in the competition. His words slipped off me without wounding me and seemed utterly derisory in comparison with the emotions stirred that day. He was hurt when he realised that his reprimands had not produced the desired effect, and he took advantage of the incident to lay bare his grievances as a neglected husband. He sensed that I was elsewhere, far, far away, and accused me of avoiding his presence, of holing up for hours on end in my studio. His asymmetrical moustaches quivered; not a good sign. He had applied for a job when the government had started to set up a medical network in the most far-flung corners of the country. Generations of healers, blacksmiths and other quacks glanced sceptically at the new recruits. Still, Konya, the granary of the country, needed doctors, obstetricians and proper dentists. A dentist's surgery was awaiting him.

Difficult though it was to remain untouched by his enthusiasm, the news that one of my nearest and dearest had died could not have grieved me more. He handed me the missive with the seal of the Republic of Turkey, making the same gesture as my son Nedim when he proffered his scribbles to me. My lips made a superhuman effort to congratulate him. I was a ruin, filled with the debris that had fallen from my walls with a muffled roar; he was an unassailable fortress. My artillery was paltry compared to his, my lines of writing powerless in the face of this enforced exile.

Ceri had sensed my sadness. Pretending to feel guilty, he sang the praises of the cultural opportunities of Konya, an old stop-over on the caravan routes and a place of pilgrimage. According to him, the sanctuary there was stuffed to overflowing with calligraphic compositions.

We would be living in a typical town house, next to the old *medersa* of Karatay that had been turned into a museum in 1927. The dervishes, fanatical opponents of Atatürk, had deserted the town and the whole area, leaving behind them the insistent music of the *ney*[18] and the viola. Their phantoms continued to spin on their left heels in a ritual dance. They chose places in which they could exhibit their skills in such a way as to be visible to everyone, then disappeared into the sandstone cliffs of the Anatolian steppe. One of them paid me a spectacular visit; the palm of his hand turned up, he gathered the grace of the heavens and transmitted it to earth. His spinning hypnotised me so much that I did not see him go. His spectre slipped away as if by miracle, after seeking the best corner of the room to prepare for his flight: an unusual way of welcoming me. And a reception granted to me alone. Government envoys were not given the same privilege.

Ceri set up his surgery near the town's *hammam**. On the opening day, a long, winding queue stretched back to the stalls of the bazaar. The oldest men stood at the head, followed by women and children. The latter caused havoc in the crowd and improvised games to while away the time. Ceri asked the men to come back the next day; the queue was reduced by half. He treated over forty patients on the first day, and attracted even

---

* Turkish steam bath. [Tr.]

more as his reputation grew. Every evening, he would report all the rumours going round town to me, especially the scandals.

He described in detail the thunderbolt of 1901 that had destroyed the slender minaret of the *medersa*. This natural catastrophe had been perceived by believers as a punishment from God. Ceri also told me that the blind man who used to recount the history of the Seljuks[19] on the square had perfectly good sight, and that old Bâkî lived a little away from the village, in a house stuffed full of talismans and amulets. Even the worst pain could not hold out against his ointments composed of a mixture of herbs and animal greases. Bâkî's cupping glasses got rid of aches, spasms and sprains. A doctor and a seer. He could read the future in the flesh of a fish from the Caspian Sea. Ceri despised this pseudo-doctor and called him a sorcerer. When he lit the lights for Shabbat[20] or Hanukkah,[21] his neighbours would turn to heaven and beg a benevolent saint to protect them. The Ramadan fast lasted a month, his for just a day. And how amazed his neighbours were, too, when he lapsed into silence every Friday evening, not lighting any lamps, not heating up any food, refusing all visits. Some of the village people were tempted to adopt this attractive custom, but the theologian from the *medersa* forbad them to. He taxed them with impiety.

Their naivety touched Ceri, who would talk about them in the same terms as an ethnologist discovering a primitive tribe.

My husband's days were very full compared to mine, which were divided between monitoring Nedim's lessons and seeing the wives of various notables. These spouses were very mistrustful towards me; the women of Istanbul were real hussies in their view.

I would cover my head and shoulders with a veil and visit the religious institutions of the town, entering the sanctuaries, which I observed with the eyes of a calligrapher. The former lodge of the whirling dervishes had just been transformed into a museum. The man in charge of historical monuments, Murat, was my guide in this place that had once been open to pilgrims. He led me to the Basin of April, filled with the sacred rains that assured one of a cure, fertility and long life.

At home I could always sense the presence of the departed dervishes. They came to inspect the state of their former abode. The inert air expressed their confusion. Stirred by whirling bodies, it could make the dance of the white robes and the red felt hats go faster or slower. Frozen into place, the robes were turned into shrouds, and the hats into steles. The dervishes were sorry about the air, which deserved a better fate.

On these heights, the spring was accompanied by a burning wind that spoke in a strange voice. I could not understand these vociferations, nor read between its gusts. It swept across the tall hummocks of grass to the main road as if to indicate the route I should take, urged me to leave the town that its servants had deserted – a town that had once been a place where the Prophet had stayed and was now laid open to tourists. The spring would call me through the shutters and then come banging on my windowpanes. It breathed a warm wind at the start of April, and the snowcap on the mountain summit melted all at once. The plateau was again verdant. My heart, which had turned to stone, was again filled with warmth and freedom.

I left Ceri behind me, left the mud of Konya, the red earth of the freshly ploughed furrows and the ghosts of the dervishes hovering over their lost fiefdom. Nedim went back with me. The Bosphorus and our ancestral dwelling awaited us. I was supposed to be coming back to Konya at the start of the autumn, but this season vanished forever from the calendar of my memory.

I felt like a negligent wife and I tried to salve my bad conscience by cleaning the house in Beylerbey from top to bottom; it had been unoccupied for months. Not a speck of dust would resist me! I took down curtains and hangings and proceeded to wash them energetically. My hands plunged into soapy mixtures, moved to the rhythm of brushes, dishcloths and clothes pegs. While I was at it I also tidied away useless bits and pieces and bitter memories: chipped plates, odd glasses, wedding photos and all of Ceri's clothes. I flung them into an old suitcase and shut them away in a locked and closed bedroom – the coldest and darkest room in the house.

Once I had tidied the house, I attacked the shed and transformed it into a studio. Two bay windows would dispense light to my tools.

The slimy mud of the riverbank rejoiced to see me laying renewed siege to these places and stirring the dust from cellar to attic. Nedim ran from our house to my parents' *yali* a few yards away, the only one that had kept its red paint from the beginning of the century. It was not long before old Selim came to pay me a visit. He made his entrance showing off every trick he could think of, flying in at a low altitude, looping the loop again and again to arouse my admiration. It was a dazzling display that he knew off by heart, a turn he must have perfected during my long months of exile in Konya. His territory was limited, as Selim did not have the right to venture any further than the Bosphorus, and especially not as far as the steppes of Anatolia, an area that came within the jurisdiction of hell.

His hand, impatient to pick up his instruments again, trembled when he saw them. He should have lost that tremble by cutting the wood of the cypress trees of the Beyond, an exercise supposed to stiffen the over-relaxed ligaments of his hand – a hand that he turned to the moon to receive its benefits.

Seeing him, I could not fail to think of the other old men from the *medersa*. Were they still in this world? Had they died natural deaths or had they been given a helping hand?

My visit to the *medersa* filled me with horror. The rooms were filthy, the walls soot-blackened. Prostrate in the corners, my old friends had a vacant gaze; even madness no longer dared to approach them. Nobody provided them with the equipment they needed for their work. They uttered unintelligible words as they dragged their bony bodies around. Mehmet amused himself by undressing from bottom to top, scrupulously folding his clothes, and then repeating the exercise in the opposite order. As they no longer had any notion of space or time, others among them thought that six months had gone by in a single day. They did not recognise me. The intrusion of a woman did not disturb them; Murad, the one who was a hundred years old, continued to declaim the verses of the Koran like the imam from his *minbar*:[22]

> *By the Pen, and what they inscribe,*
> *thou art not, by the blessing of thy Lord,*
> *a man possessed.*[23]

His sermon had no impact on his colleagues. Nobody bothered to listen to his words of wisdom. One of them even tried to slap him in the face; Murad's finger as it pointed at him was a provocation, an insult.

I choked back my tears.

Was I in the sieve of purgatory? I waited with a lump in my throat for God to bear them off to His paradise.

The corridors of the *medersa* seemed quite empty to me – they had been deserted ever since the National Academy of Fine Arts opened its doors to new recruits. Several calligraphers were now teachers there. According to Rahmi the bicycle seller, who was now also, on the side, the curator of the old monument (by 'curator' I mean he swept the floor and gathered up the dead leaves), the new educational institution had started to give itself the airs of a Western university. The teachers dressed like Europeans and the end of each class was marked by a bell that was noisier than the chant of the muezzin from the neighbouring mosque. He told me about a woman candidate who had taken part in the calligraphy competition the previous year; she had vanished without saying why, though she had won the first prize. Some said that she was dead, others thought that her father had locked her away in the latrines of his house. The competition organisers had not made much of an effort to give her the good news, for fear of offending an angry father or husband. Without realising it, Rahmi was talking about me.

Necmeddin Okyay, a great calligrapher, was both imam at the Yeni Djami Mosque and a gardener. His house was just like him: discreet, with an attic room whose ceiling was as low as his back when he bent down over his roses to sniff their fragrance. He was madly in love with these flowers, and knew by heart the botanical names of four hundred species of them, and an equal number of verses of the Koran, which he would recite in a grave voice. He gave me a warm welcome and introduced his roses to me one after the other, like a sultan presenting his concubines.

He moved on straight away to ask me why I had disappeared after the competition. My answer was as evasive as the attention he paid it. He reminded me that he had, on that particular day, tried to prop up my desk. My absence had fuelled the most extravagant rumours. My composition had been hung up in the entrance hall of the Academy.

Necmeddin's remarks were punctuated by short prayers, meant to draw Allah's benefits down on me. I followed him in his peregrinations through the rose garden. Each flower had the right to a blessing. The philanthropic gardener was convinced that talent is a gift that can be shared and transmitted. Allah distributes, and we redistribute in turn, until the world's end – so he affirmed in the tones of a preacher. Necmeddin's hands rose repeatedly to the heavens and towards the Creator who, in his sacred somnolence, dictated the right words to him when he flattered the pride of his roses, while at the same time putting him on his guard against the grafts inspired by the Devil. His garden would remain under the protection of Allah, who would turn back storms and cut off the rays of the sun until his flowers had reached the lower tip of his ear lobe. Faithful to the divine observances, Necmeddin was merely the spokesman of the Most Great, a small patch of his shadow upon the earth. I suspected that he was not really interested in me – hence the brutal way he brought our visit to an end, doubtless eager to take up his clippers again, in league with the lunar months.

Our conversation ended in an exchange of politely proffered formulae.

On the way home, my feet as they trod on the pebbles made a noise as of modest thanks. I had set my sights on a job as a teacher, and my efforts were rewarded, thus allaying any sense of guilt towards Ceri, who was impatient for me to return to Konya. After a month, his tone turned threatening. The word 'separation' reared its head without my having to pronounce it. In my eyes he was a stranger; perhaps he had never ceased to be one. I left him with a feeling of relief.

I took up my work again with a sort of jubilation. My margins overflowed with flowery foliage, with tulips, eglantines, roses and carnations whose every petal I drew with precision. They blossomed rapidly; no bulb could resist my hand, nourished with manure and ink. My paper smelled of damp earth and the early morning dew. I would water the composition, trim the useless stalks and the withered petals.

My tools rejoiced at the idea of officiating in front of my future pupils, and the ink had to stop salivating when the official summons to the Academy arrived. The interview was arranged for a late afternoon in a room reserved for teachers. Ismail Hakki, the competition organiser, spoke first. His questions betrayed the mistrust he felt for a woman who was trying to get into a profession usually reserved for men. There were technical questions concerning the way calligraphic materials were prepared, and then some further ones about my erudition in matters of religion. Old Selim enjoyed prompting me with the answers, and the members of the appointments committee were surprised to see me revealing secrets of calligraphic production that had been kept inside the studios for centuries. My mixtures contained unknown substances from plants that no longer existed, juices from rodents that were dying out, or spices with strange names that had been used by the pagan peoples of bygone days. My concoctions smelled of age-old soot, the acidic odours of potters' ovens, the sweat or emanations of immolated sheep. The imaginary vapours of white lead, vinegar, or camphor-based ferments rose to Selim's nostrils as he saw his years as a young apprentice and the warnings of his teacher pass before his eyes. That old madman slipped his secrets to me, and I disclosed them in a tone worthy of the Ten Commandments:

Take equal weights of alum and of soot,
The double of the gall of oak to boot,
Then thou shalt add a triple dose of gum,
And use the strength and vigour of thine arm.[24]

My words so perplexed them that they had to confer before reaching a decision. Ismail Hakki asked his colleagues to go back to their places and delivered his verdict. His voice was solemn in tone. My concoctions and my expressions struck them as archaic, and certain of my ingredients would be unobtainable even from the best-stocked chemists' shops. Nonetheless, my knowledge of my subject justified my admission to the Academy.

Their congratulations were mingled with bitterness; they put me on my guard against the illusions of the *métier*. It was not easy to be a calligrapher these days; printing, and then the Latin alphabet imposed by Atatürk, had hardly enabled the profession to prosper. The presses worked relentlessly, even during Ramadan. Letters in lead had no difficulty in moving from inspiration to expiration. We calligraphers, however, held our breath when we traced our letters and breathed again when the *qalam* dipped its tip into the inkpot. They told me of the uprising and the militants' march that had been organised in the streets a few years earlier, when a coffin filled with *qalams* had been borne aloft.

Only my husband's rebukes, forever harassing me in his letters, cast a shadow over my happiness. But his disappointment was of little weight compared to the encouragements of the Academy. My investiture enabled me to gain the favours of a great Ottoman woman calligrapher who had died a century previously. Esma Ibret Hanim, a pupil of the great Mahmud Celaleddin Efendi, traced her name in letters of light on the walls of my moonlit bedroom. A fine gold dust, like the one she scattered over her calligraphies, made the room glimmer. I had been given the protection of two calligraphers: such was the conclusion I drew. Esma felt at home in my *yali*, situated not far from her house in Istavroz where she looked out over the same quarter of the moon. Sitting on the Asian shore of the Bosphorus, Beylerbey enjoyed a fine reputation among calligraphers, since the alphabet had first trodden on Asian soil.

She signalled me to take up a *qalam*, and designated a sheet of paper by raising it slightly with a breath of air. She moved back the chair from my desk so as to sit me down on it, placed the inkpot to the right of the paper, and the support for the *qalam* just beneath. Her desire to communicate with me mobilised the joints of my fingers. The *qalam* reawoke and plunged its head into the ink to wash its face; then it set to work without flinching. I recognised the letters as she dictated them to me and, guessing the word, I hurried to write it down. She was vexed at my haste and challenged me to start again, savoured each letter and made the points and vowel signs dance. Anxious to improve my work, she set my wrist in the correct position, smoothed out an over-tense finger, made me unbend my hunched shoulders. The dead can sometimes be very authoritarian. Esma had been roughly treated by her master, and knew of no other way to teach. Her master, a stubborn and tyrannical man, was never satisfied with her work. He was always finding fault, and put on a wounded expression when she presented her compositions to him. The old calligrapher had been redoing, for the hundredth time, a line that was not upright enough for her master's taste, when she had succumbed to a violent seizure. Weary of seeing her forever struggling and sighing, God had chosen this moment to call her to him. Her last breath made her pencil skid on the paper, leaving a wobbly streak. Esma left this world horrified at the sight, regretting that she would not be able to erase this last stroke.

On the evening of her visit, she corrected several times over a character that was on the point of making a hole in my page. I was so curious to know what would come next that my fingers skipped the tear and pursued their odyssey. My eyes discovered these lines:

Calligraphers never die. Their souls wander around on the frontiers of the inhabited word seeking to retrieve their instruments. God uses them to reveal his word. Prophets proclaim it, calligraphers write it down.

I aspire to eternal rest but he has not granted it to me. He does not know that badly formed letters assail me, that imperfect shapes torture me and that the architecture of a line depends on the air contained within our lungs. We, the dead, have no breath left. Forming letters gives us well-being and plenitude; the Beyond does not allow us to use our hands.

I left this world without having tasted the perfection of an immaculate piece of work or an ideal composition.

Help me to forget the vertical strokes and ligatures of the letters that torment me even in my sleep.

Esma Ibret had transgressed the laws of the Beyond. Nobody was authorised to reveal the whys and wherefores of the place of eternal repose. I could understand old Selim's visits better – his practical jokes and his magic tricks. Selim, a comical ghost, had not yet had the time to get bored by this half-death reserved for calligraphers – while Esma on the other hand, wearied by her peculiar status, wanted to die once and for all.

God is not interested in the Latin alphabet. His dense breath cannot skim across those squat, separate letters. 'Atatürk has driven God out of the country', the calligraphers kept saying. Now the Grey Wolf, the sole power-holder, an admirer of Western culture, an enemy of illiteracy, had reformed writing, the same way one replaces mother's milk with the artificial variety. Arabic–Persian words had been eliminated, to be replaced by Turkish words. The new language had eight phonetic vowels, where Arabic has only three, and the letters were no longer linked together. Characters no longer carried any accents, and letters no longer changed their shape depending on their position in their phrase. Now we wrote from left to right. It is said that linguistic specialists asked Atatürk for five years to draw up an alphabet: he granted them just three months.

Calligraphers were sorely wounded, and so was the Koran. The Arabic language was banned from all public usage and the suras were no longer taught in the schools. We no longer told time by the sun; instead, we used the international method with a twenty-four-hour clock.

Men appointed by the Linguistic Commission went round the villages, collecting the elements that belonged to the lexicon of Turkish, cleansing our language of its Arabic–Persian vocabulary, scrutinising our inner hearts, lending an ear to family quarrels, listening to the peasant calling to his cattle and the lover asking for the hand of his beloved in marriage.

The old Arabic terms were sometimes replaced by French words, which young people enjoyed declaiming in Western style. We even changed our family names; I was no longer Rikkat, daughter of Necib bey, nor the wife of Ceri Ince, but Rikkat Kunt, a name that I made up for myself and that I was the only person to bear.

My family circumstances were of little interest to the members of the Academy; calligraphers are often unmarried since they dedicate their lives to Allah. I was separated from Ceri, bringing up my seven-year-old son alone; it was a subject they preferred not to broach and I was grateful to them for this. Calligraphers are hybrid beings, neither men nor women, which is why God keeps them close to himself. This priesthood curbs their desire for offspring; the only dynasties of calligraphies that endure through the centuries are those that issue from unions arranged between young apprentices and the daughters of their masters. In this way the inheritance remains intact. A few newborns are already lying in their cradles becoming familiar with the tube of bamboo that, later on, they will dip into ink. Their plump little wrists learn how to handle a *qalam* very early on. They improvise all sorts of games; they create affinities with time.

The blood of calligraphers is different from that of other human beings: it grows dark on contact with ink, and their wounds dry more quickly. Calligraphers write within themselves and then offer a partial vision of their flesh, blackened by the alphabet. They are said to be very secretive, but they are simply extremely modest and reticent about revealing their anatomy. The words of the Most High are never written well enough. Calligraphers need to die before they can hear his indecipherable voice and his untranslatable words. The dead – they say – have good ears, to make up for their lack of good eyes.

In what alphabet does God express himself? Certainly not in the Latin alphabet – so I was assured by Muhsin, my closest friend at the Academy. The new generation of calligraphers was embarking on a really rather strange profession, since they were strictly forbidden to write in Arabic. Our rooms at the Academy were used to teach the people in our district to read and write; they would repeat in unison the letters pronounced by the teacher.

Our avid hands would seek consolation by tracing spirals of vegetation, which would sometimes adopt the curves of this or that Arabic consonant hidden behind a malicious rosebud. When sleep would not come, my fingers grazed the starched grain of my sheets and drew the quatrains of an old poem over and over again, until they were exhausted. Muhsin would try to resist, but the temptation was too great, and he would write verses of the Koran on the misted-up windowpanes of his bedroom, while a kettle steamed constantly on the stove. We could not stop imagining the forbidden letters on a bare wall, on a cloudy sky or an empty plate.

Ismail Hakki, our master, found a remedy that would make it easier for us to wean ourselves; deploring the state of the historical documents conserved at Topkapi[25] and in the old libraries of the Ottoman sultans, he was given permission by the Republic of Turkey to repair works that were five centuries old.

We were to restore documents that lay rolled up in forgotten corners, try and work out the ingredients of age-old inks, and reconstitute the illuminated decorations in margins devoured by whole families of rats. The flesh of the letters had become bony, and the dust covering certain sheets of paper was like the ashes of funeral urns. We had no access to the works preserved in the palace treasure, but only to those of lesser importance from the old offices of the chancellery. But this was enough for our happiness to be assured. The creation of the Topkapi Museum in 1924 had in any case spared the former from the injuries of time, while thousands of others awaited the same treatment in the basements of the city's monuments. In this way, several Korans, fascicles of Korans and certificates of pilgrimage that had been kept for centuries in the libraries of the Empire were transferred. Some were discovered in the *Hasoda*,[26] the Library of Hagia Sophia, or in the many pious endowments[27] that had been closed down on Atatürk's orders, and in a few mosques and mausoleums of the great religious complexes.

We examined them meditatively, moved by the sight of so much care and effort, and tried to translate the signatures of eminent calligraphers that had once been active in the palace studios. That of Ahmed Karahisari, the master calligrapher of Suleiman the Magnificent, who died at the age of ninety, was particularly difficult to identify. And yet his great age had not diminished the skill of his hand or the precision of his ornamentation. He saw me struggling so hard to decipher his name that he gave me a severe reprimand. His rebukes were uttered in the noblest Ottoman dialect. This long-dead man, close to the great Suleiman, could not speak to women except in authoritarian tones. A profoundly misogynistic man, he mocked my ignorance and deemed it quite unacceptable that I could not read his name inscribed on the colophon of a prayer book.

Insults, sometimes coarse, escaped from the lips of this ghost whose breath had an odour of earth. His visit was a change from the burlesque apparitions of old Selim or my encounters with the engaging Esma Ibret Hanim. Since I could not in all decency return his insults, I turned a deaf ear and stopped paying any attention to his attacks. He vanished, disappointed that he had not managed to make me cry.

Calligraphers have such changeable moods. I was starting to get used to their complex personalities and their frequent visits.

My hand was breaking up the letters, but the *qalam* kept slipping out of my hands. I managed to discipline it in the straight bits, but it twisted and turned like an acrobat in the convex and concave lines.

Just as it came into contact with the sheet of paper, the row of signs was interrupted by a harsh scratching noise. I grasped it firmly between index finger and thumb, and held it at an angle, but the arc of a circle that it drew was sheered sideways by an invisible force. I returned to my initial position and traced out a *mim* in the *diwani* style;[28] the outline trembled and my breath, instead of drying up the letter, effaced it like a wave on the sand. The slanting section of my reed split and turned into a powder like saffron dust. The cover of my inkpot snapped shut without asking my permission, as if my tools wanted to tell me something. I would have to seek the reasons for their mutiny elsewhere. It did not bode well.

This is how the Most High generally announces the death of someone close to the calligrapher. The latter then has to work out who is meant. The *qalams* are never wrong, they shrug off responsibility.

My father's death was just like him. Illness forced him to keep to his bed for several months. He was a rich merchant, accustomed to power relations, and he submitted to death with a schoolboy's obedience after a long resistance.

He shifted the position of his bed and placed it behind the door so that he would be better able to see when Azrael, the Angel of Death, arrived. He awaited him every night, wide-eyed, holding a rifle longer than his bed that he had inherited from a great-great-uncle, a former janissary of Sultan Abdülmecid. He did not envisage that Azrael would take him by surprise in the middle of the day, as he was recovering from one of his restless nights, and he just had time to summon me to his bedside.

He spoke to me in a murmur. He was anxious about the turn my life was taking. He found my profession a strange one, since I could not practise it, and my marriage a melancholy business, since I could not consummate it. I had not seen Ceri for five months, and yet I had not missed him for a single minute. 'The situation can't continue like this, you need to do something,' he made me promise. 'Nedim mustn't suffer from having immature parents. And what about your work – what does it consist of? In writing a forbidden language or invoking a God who's been thrown out?'

I saw his face darken; would God be there to welcome him, or had he deserted this secular country so that he would not even receive its dead any more?

Our conversation came to an end on this note of anguish. He would rather have died in Aleppo at his old sister's, but he should have made arrangements earlier.

I left his room accompanied by the click of the beads on his rosary as he counted them off, uttering the ninety-nine names of Allah. He succumbed at the hundredth bead, the one that exists only in paradise.

There were thirty of us at his funeral, standing in a circle around his coffin, wishing him eternal rest. Rich grain merchants from the Balkans or Macedonia, the neighbours, and a few friends. Ceri had come to comfort me and, while he was here, to see his son, whom he had not set eyes on for five months. My bereavement made this confrontation easier and we agreed to divorce. To my great surprise, he announced that he had come to Istanbul to make the same suggestion to me. Ceri was planning to start a new life with a teenage girl from Anatolia who was in a great hurry to marry. He promised our son that he would see him again when he returned to Istanbul to replenish his stocks of dentist's equipment.

Ceri was a respected notable in Konya, but he had never before come across a wild-eyed dervish and his prayers repeated in unison.

We were just leaving the cemetery when an enigmatic character who seemed not to know anyone there came up to introduce himself. He was too upset to offer his condolences in the proper manner, and merely whispered his name. He had met my father during a stay in Albania, and enjoyed talking to him about political events in the region. Both of them were supporters of King Zog, and worried by Italy's colonial ambitions. Their conversations had become more infrequent lately, as my father's paralysing migraines had cut him off from the world. Mehmet Fahreddin, born in Tirana, had the manner of a Western diplomat, and went so far as to copy the accent; he also dressed in European style. He was a member of the court of King Zog, and gave himself the airs of a political adviser who had come to deliver confidential messages of the highest importance. His numerous trips to Europe, especially France, had been an opportunity for him to improve his knowledge of politics and economics, and he recycled bits and pieces of his expertise in salon conversations. His analyses and subtle aperçus quite seduced his audience.

My father's death had deprived him of an admirer, and he unwittingly sought to conquer our family now that it lacked a masculine authority figure. Each time he came to town, he would pay us long visits, always refusing to stay to dinner, but always yielding, in the end, to our pressing invitations. His comings and goings between Istanbul and Tirana became more and more frequent; eventually we placed a room at his disposal, and it soon smelled strongly of his eau de Cologne, imported from Europe. He would leave very early in the morning, as the promiscuity of breakfast made him feel ill at ease, and come back in the evening, shattered. He was a great hit with the whole family and soon became one of us; only young Nedim did not really like his aristocratic airs. His activities seemed strange to us, and the thought sometimes crossed our minds that we were sheltering a spy who had come to glean state secrets. He seemed flattered when we confided these suspicions to him, and did not attempt to deny them.

In the spring of 1939, he resided in our house for over a month. Italy had infiltrated Albania, indeed had completely invaded the country, and King Zog had taken refuge in Greece with his family; Mehmet Fahreddin took refuge with us, where he was safe from privations and war.

His status in our household evolved rapidly; our bedrooms opened up to one another at nightfall and the spy was transformed into a clandestine lover. Mehmet cultivated this clandestine role skilfully, right up to the day my divorce came through. He was impatient to marry and acquire Turkish nationality, so he bribed the people in the Beylerbey town hall to make our marriage official as quickly as possible. The portrait of Atatürk darted a disapproving glance at us. Mehmet had asked the owner of the *yali* next door to be his witness; my witness was my younger sister, Hateme.

My new husband always chose key dates to express his affection to me. He made his first declaration of love on the day Atatürk died, 10th November 1938, and our son, Ahmet Nurullah, was conceived on 3rd September 1939, the day on which Britain and France declared war on Germany. Now that his political ambitions had been reduced to ashes, he liked to establish symbolic parallels between his life and history; he was delighted that he had been born on 3rd April 1905, the date on which a meteor had chosen a trajectory close to our planet.

We were an ideally hospitable land for him – and warmhearted hosts. The country observed strict neutrality during the war. We were the inhabitants of a land held in suspense, standing apart from the conflicts, inert until the earthquake of 27th December 1939. This seismic shock, registering eight on the Richter scale, caused the death of thirty thousand people and affected the whole of Turkey. An earthquake as destructive as aerial bombardments... This subterranean punishment occurred during my pregnancy, and it was to have repercussions on the destiny of my second son. Tossed around from one country to another, Nour would never find a firm footing on any soil. The strange thing is that the only country that made him happy, namely France, was bombarded, on the day he was born, by three hundred German planes, and finally surrendered on 14th June 1940, when Hitler's army entered Paris.

The enemy was on our frontiers. On 6th April 1941, Germany attacked Yugoslavia and Greece. Their bombers did not venture any further. All the same, we could sometimes hear the German patrols turning back.

In spite of our neutrality, the conflict had damaged the country's economy. The regime grew more rigid and Islam came back onto the political scene. It is a well-known fact that religions emerge in times of war. The whole world was going up in flames, and rumours of massacres and genocides came to our ears. Prayer was our sole shield.

On 27 Ramadan,[29] a night on which the destiny of every being is fixed, the whole country turned to God and implored him to return to earth. The men brought out their prayer carpets, the women repeated the *bismillah* all day long. Religious broadcasts on the radio urged everyone to pray and encouraged them to undertake the pilgrimage to Mecca. Small craftsmen and itinerant merchants again filled the streets with the clatter of their asses' hooves. The religious schools reopened their heavy wooden shutters. Streets and houses were filled with fervour, while memories of the secular Atatürk continued to dominate people's minds.

I awoke my instruments from their long sleep, and old Selim's inkpot returned to its place on my table. My fingers, swollen by my pregnancy, grasped the *qalam* more firmly. The baby's kicks made my lines swerve this way and that and transformed my letters into keen-edged sabres. The result was not without charm. The father read in them his son's artistic leanings. However, the boy would later prefer the staves of his musical theory exercise book to the heavy, unmusical writings of his mother's sketches.

My mother impatiently awaited her second grandson. We had not dared to choose a name for him; the Devil might have stolen him from me. According to the woman next door, it was in the first months after conception that the embryo received the four divine decisions: food, lifespan, happiness and unhappiness. But Mehmet refused to believe it; he despised these superstitions and tore off the amulets that I hung by the cradle.

Nurullah was born one April morning after a night of painful labour. My mother picked up the placenta and buried it under a tree in the garden. 'He's got a big head; baby's going to be clever,' said the midwife. His father did not conceal his pride. The cries of his son were signs of vitality. He called him 'little Nour' or 'little light'.

When night fell, he sent us away and sat down by his cradle to tell him the story of the great men of his native land. The story of Mehmet Ali, the adventurer, an old tobacco merchant who had become the leader of the Albanian troops in the Turkish army, or the story of the revolutionary Skanderberg. His ecstatic language made the baby jump. My mother and sister drove him out of the bedroom to quieten the little boy's tears by singing him a lullaby. His father responded the very next day by telling him all about the exploits of Tamerlane the Great or 'the lame man of iron' who had lined up pyramids of skulls. He vaunted these massacres with shining eyes, and the corners of his lips were flecked with foam.

Mehmet took advantage of the times when his son was asleep to creep into his room and criticise the policies of Atatürk. He viewed female emancipation with displeasure, and thought it improbable that they would be given the vote, even if one day they might be eligible. He muttered away in the darkness. His sole audience was a sleeping child.

Nedim was perturbed by the birth of his brother and avoided his presence, preferring to go fishing with old Mustafa, who had been mute ever since a bad dentist in Beylerbey had torn his jaw out along with his teeth. They would wait for a bite for hours on end, rocked by the rhythm of the waves that swelled as the big liners from the Black Sea sailed by. None of us could stand my husband's monologues. The tortoise preferred to drown itself in the pond rather than put up with his speeches. This suicide saddened us.

At table we would launch into absolutely any subject so as to interrupt his diatribes. He was against everything and everyone, he condemned the banning of the veil and the prohibition of polygamy. His sleep was just like his waking hours; he would start up a debate with his eyes closed, expressing the ideas that had been censored during the day and plotting underhand reprisals against the women in the family.

Mehmet always ended up being left by himself. Everyone avoided him, even young Lale, who did the household ironing. She pretended to be deaf and mute so as to avoid his lectures. But two ears, even if they were deaf, were all he needed. One day Lale picked up her wages and disappeared, never to return.

Peace and quiet became a rare commodity in the house. I took advantage of the night to stock up on silence, and worked then in spite of the walls that swayed, the floorboards that creaked and the fireplaces that breathed with the wind. Our *yali* was getting old; my mother did not have the wherewithal to restore it. My husband had even less money – he had nothing but contempt for those who worked for a living. The Bosphorus had been eroding our foundations for years; its spray made the windows opaque, and my mother aged as fast as the *yali* turned into a ruin. She was nostalgic for the past, and she had found in cleanness an ally for her sadness.

Each and every object made her lapse into a contemplative silence. Her life passed before her eyes whenever she saw an old perfume bottle from Beykoz, a little mat she had embroidered at the age of sixteen, or our father's handkerchiefs that had been starched a thousand times.

She kept saying that if she gave everything a really thorough polish, it would make her memories even more precise.

She remembered her years as a rich city girl and her beauty, famed as far afield as the villages next to Beylerbey.

Nour's cries would all too quickly bring her back to reality. He wanted to touch everything and amused himself ransacking the knick-knacks in the living room. The only thing he could not get his hands on was the collection of ceramics from Iznik presented by Sultan Selim III to his *gözde*,[30] my great-aunt, the jewel of his harem. Spurned by his successor Mustafa IV, she had been transferred to the Eski Saray[31] where she had passed away all alone. It was a sumptuous collection: *tabak*,[32] *bardak*[33] and *masrapa*[34] were lit up by the rays of the setting sun. On the same shelf, my mother had placed the *berat*[35] drawn up by the Sultan's chancellery; the name of her father, who had been responsible for collecting taxes and transferring them to the treasury, was written there in full. She was particularly proud of this document, which she had stopped hoisting up on the wall ever since Atatürk had taken power.

I remember that when I was a girl I enjoyed tracing the interwoven pattern of the Sultan's monogram together with his patronymic and the epithet 'ever-victorious'. I imagined the sovereign, with his pot belly, sitting in the lotus position on his throne, a big diamond pinned to his turban and his two arms dangling limply either side of the armrests. Copying the Sultan's *tughra* over and over was my favourite pastime; my father, who was worried about forgeries, warned me off this practice in spite of the precision of my copies that could deceive the most expert eye. He urged me rather to reproduce the 'waves and rocks' designs on the raised rim of our ceramic plates or the famous *qi* clouds dear to the Chinese. I worked so hard at it that he eventually hired a drawing teacher, an old maid from Bebek, a small village on the western shore of the Bosphorus. My father had to go and fetch her and then take her back home, since the transport vessels attracted – she said – the wrong sort of people. Kösem, who had lived for three years in Florence, was a dedicated supporter of the Italian *maniera* and worshipped Bellini fanatically. In Kösem's eyes, the light of Venice was comparable with that of our good old Constantinople, and the Adriatic was a cousin of our Bosphorus.

She would absent-mindedly dip her paintbrush into her cup of apple tea, and drink the (now multicoloured) rinsing water.

Her lessons made a point of the links between art and the wars waged by bloodthirsty sultans. Had not Selim I, at the sack of

Tabriz, enriched his collections with Chinese porcelains, pieces which influenced the artists of the *nakkashane*[36]? And had not the Iranian war-captives from the court of Herat brought Timurid and Safavid designs that our Anatolian hands had gone on to develop? Kösem had a passion for Chinese drawings, which she copied into a sketchbook. Each page was dedicated to a particular theme: the *saz* palm,[37] *hatayi* flowers,[38] *hanceri* leaves,[39] and *cintimani* decorations,[40] which I in turn copied in detail, plants from the forests on the borders of Central Asia and China, a flora that concealed laughing faces, and rocks with human profiles observing the landscape with their wide open eyes. With all the expertise of his two years of age, Nour already had well-defined tastes. He could recognise the stylised tulips that he touched with his finger as if he wanted to strip the leaves off them. Then there was the thoughtful expression on his face when turned to the Mecca drawn on a ceramic tile. He scrutinised the cube with its swathes of gilt. The Kaaba, his father had told him, shelters the black stone of men's sins; they go round it the same way that the earth turns round the sun. But Nour preferred my drawing to the explanations; the stone thirty centimetres in diameter, coloured black and heightened here and there in red and yellow, fascinated him. He was grateful to me every time that I spared him the long paternal sermons.

To his childish eyes, Mecca was a place of amusement, in which a crowd went round and round a puppet show like the one in Karagoz.

We experienced the war vicariously, as the radio informed us of the latest German breakthroughs and the atrocities revealed after so many years of silence.

Still wearing his most elegant suit, my husband would wander along the shores of the Bosphorus, pulling greedily on his pipe. The war had killed off his ambitions, dried up his eloquence, and ruined our already fragile life together. Only the chuckles of our son would provide us with any semblance of harmony.

My old mother watched our fortune melting away before her eyes. Mehmet refused the positions he was offered. Considering himself to be far superior to all these proposals, he turned down a job as curator of the Istanbul library, and another one as an assistant city planner in the city. His political ruminations fuelled his megalomaniac ravings to such a point that the family placed an entire wing of the house at his disposal so as not to have to hear his alarmist prophecies and his visionary warnings.

These tensions were pent up until that wretched day... One day, as I was writing Koranic verses in *gubari*,[41] Mehmet came in without knocking, overturned the inkpot on the squared sheets of paper, picked up old Selim's *divit* and hurled it through the studio window. He left without a word. Nedim tried in vain to fish the object out, but the Bosphorus had swallowed it. Awoken by the noise, old Selim must have decided that the mud was more to his taste than the dry earth of his burial place, and he recovered what belonged to him. The writing case was never found.

I imagined the inkpot and the *qalams* wrapped in damp earth, swayed this way and that by the currents, and my heart contracted.

The house suddenly became silent. The only sound was that of Nour's voice as he recited the alphabet. His father said he was waiting for the war to end so that he could leave this waste land and this family of simpletons. We too were looking forward to the cessation of conflict, impatient to resume possession of our house that had been split in two by a line of demarcation – the only boundary that could ensure our peace and quiet.

The capitulation of Germany in May 1945 was not enough to make him decide to leave. His mania for linking his life to the great events in the world made him hold out until 6th August, the day when the United States decided to drop a bomb on Hiroshima. The bomb exploded forty-five seconds later. My husband took just as long to walk out of our lives once and for all. He accepted a post as manager of the tobacco factory in Beirut, on the one condition that he would take his son with him. I can still see Nour following his father, struggling under the weight of the suitcase filled to overflowing with his lead soldiers and his shells, not to mention his clothes. He thought he would be seeing us again soon, and forgot to kiss me goodbye. I held back my tears. I was weeping inside, but not uttering the slightest lament. The departure of my little light had darkened the sky. I can still see all three of us, my mother, my sister and myself, standing at the door, and there he is, waving his little hand, happy to be setting off on his travels.

This departure had been brought forward due to an incident that had happened the previous day and caused us the greatest consternation. I hesitate to relate it. Perhaps I will divulge it one day when the shame of the scandal is less bitter.

Dear Mother,

The Lebanese postal service is unreliable. I hope this letter reaches you. My father agreed to give me your address. His memory is playing tricks with him, and he made a super-human effort to recall it. Your name seems very remote, some-thing from another life. He hasn't kept any photos of you – what does my mother look like? Here and there in our albums there are cut-off photos in which my father often appears. His face has replaced yours.

He doesn't talk much. He evades all the questions I ask him about you. He manages the tobacco factory; he sent me to the Jesuits, 'the best education in the country,' he keeps saying. Is it true that I was born a Muslim? When my friends see me they prostrate themselves as if I were a descendant of the Prophet.

Life in Beirut is pleasant, but France will give me better prospects for a career. I've signed up as a medical student in Paris; classes begin next October.

I'd like to see you again, but I don't have much free time. Will you recognise me after so many years? The smell of my father's tobacco hasn't drowned out the salty breezes of the Bosphorus. Do you still have those little sculptures of dervishes on your bookshelves? I broke one when I was a child. Did you repair it?

Has Nedim got married?

With big hugs,

– Jean

I must have read this letter a hundred times, admiring the im-peccable handwriting, the sophisticated loops of the consonants and the freshness of the punctuation. My son had written it rapidly, without lingering over every detail. He had got back in touch without making too much of a fuss about it. His Christian name at the bottom of the page quite threw me. His father had decided to simplify his Muslim forename so as to make it easier for them to be integrated into a host country that was well known as the 'Switzerland of the Middle East'. He himself had ended up by taking the name Pierre. He frequented Lebanese high society, went out to social events most evenings and spent his weekends in Faraya,[42] while Nour learned the art of translating Virgil's *Aeneid*, followed the catechism classes of Father Moutran and agreed to make his first communion so as to resemble the other boys. The host had a bitter taste in his mouth compared to the round flat cakes, flavoured with thyme, that were left every morning on the doorstep of our *yali*. He chewed the body of Christ with his mouth hanging open, uneasy at the way it stuck to his palate and amazed to feel the flesh melting. Father Moutran had tied a white armband around his arm and gave him a copy of the Holy Gospels. These details were provided by my Aunt Myriam, a Turkish woman living in Syria, who wrote to me every month.

Nour's father had invented a job for himself, a post as a political advisor, an old Albanian partisan and later a close collaborator of Ismet Inonu: he claimed to be the *éminence grise* of the great men and women of this world. His popularity soon turned him into an indispensable figure; he was a guest at the best tables in the land and courted his hosts' wives. To the question 'Are you married?', his infallible sense of repartee supplied him with some very useful turns of phrase celebrating his own freedom and the beauty of the local women. His post as manager of the tobacco factory allowed him to live in a carefree style, to ensure his son had the best education, and to acquire the finest pipes imported from abroad, especially England and France. He had over seventy of them, some twenty suits and a hundred or so ties that he lovingly collected.

Father Moutran observed with sceptical eyes this 'dandy' who came to pick up his son for the summer holidays on board his pearl-grey cabriolet. The summer saw them travelling round the country, from seaside resort to seaside resort, from yacht to yacht, throwing sumptuous banquets for women in dark glasses who smoked gold-tipped cigarettes and never dipped their feet in the water. Appreciated for his eloquence and his appetite for life, Pierre became the idol of Lebanese high society. Nour would play with the children and never miss a crumb of the conversation that fell from the tables where the adults were conversing. He intercepted the adulterous glances and the secret desires, and could guess in advance what sort of woman would please his father, who liked them to be married and avid for wealth. These idylls soon fizzled out: 'those women are too expensive,' he complained to his son one day. Nour pretended not to understand. He preferred to ask questions about his mother – what was she like? But these attempts only ever produced disdainful answers about Turkish women, who were 'dangerous'. Though Nour did not possess any photo of me, he knew that I was completely different from the sophisticated Lebanese women who concealed behind their kindly appearance a fierce jealousy. His father's summertime conquests were not to his taste. In any case, the latter never followed up his charm-school act, crushed as he was by his son's contemptuous glance. Nour judged him severely.

Tired of his lovely conquests, Pierre turned to rich heiresses who were physically less attractive. Janine, the daughter of the country's biggest concrete producer, was soon won over by this seducer from foreign parts, and in spite of her father's hesitations she invited him to their property in Sofar at every opportunity. He ended up seducing the whole family, even the father, who smoked cigars with him in a room reserved for masculine conversations. After several months' worth of effort, the harvest was as generous as the dowry; Pierre asked for the young woman's hand, with the blessings of all, forgetting that his union with his Turkish wife was still valid. 'Never been married, no children: the dream-bride to start a big family with,' he said the evening before asking for her hand. Janine promised him a prosperous life to be divided between the concrete factory, the summer residence and the apartment in Beirut right next to the sea. His greed for gain had forced out his son, who was relegated to a stagnant corner of his memory. After all, his role as father could be reduced to a once-a-term visit to the boarding school – that would be enough. With his new lifestyle, he would then be able to pay for him to continue his studies at the best places in France.

The hoax worked for a few weeks until the day his fiancée unsealed a letter. She was quite disconcerted and reread it to her father, who decided the best response was to pick up the paper knife and go and slaughter that 'Levantine' who had hoaxed them.

15th June 1955

Father,

I haven't heard from you for some time. Is your work keeping you so very busy? You didn't come to the school play. I was in the role of Dr Knock. I got lots of applause. Father Antoine took photos of the performance, I'll show them to you. Father Moutran reminded me that you didn't come for Ascension Day either. 'The worst-off orphans are those who have parents still alive,' he whispered. I refuse to believe him and I hope to see you on the first day of the vacation. I'm looking forward to finding myself back in a real house, and belonging to a real family.

The summer holidays start next Saturday, I'll be standing in front of the parlour door. Don't forget me.

Your son,

– Nour

Only her father's embrace could console the betrayed fiancée. This lie would cost the guilty man dear. The father assured his daughter that it would all be settled before nightfall.

Two heavies presented themselves at the tobacco factory early that afternoon and asked to see the manager. Ali and Mustafa, Janine's father's odd-job men, sat down as if preparing for a long business negotiation. The conversation was short and to the point. Ali announced his boss's orders: Pierre was forbidden to try and see the daughter again or to come anywhere near their property. In exchange, they wouldn't reveal the reasons why the wedding was being called off. Ali's words slowed, becoming more threatening as he spoke. Pointing at the ex-fiancé, he advised him to respect these arrangements; otherwise…

The latter, completely flabbergasted, did not even have time to reply. His son's letter and the photos of the engagement, torn up and flung on the ground, made him turn pale.

Pierre came to fetch his son the following Saturday; he arrived two hours early. Father Moutran could not believe his eyes. Nour ran up to his father, swiped his hat off him, and disappeared into the depths of the car. Sitting in the driver's seat, he showed off in front of his school chums, hooting the horn.

They spent the summer together, no women, far from the social swirl. Pierre never mentioned the way his wedding had been called off, or the letter, or the rumours that were going round the town. Nour sometimes overheard people whispering and darting suspicious glances at his father, who replied with a smile.

It was a dream summer; he'd got his father back and was talking to him like an adult.

'This isn't the right country for us,' his father told him one evening.

The page lying within reach of my hand is without any surface bumps. I have lined my inkpot with a bourrette in natural sponge so as not to saturate my *qalam* with ink. Now I have only to sharpen my reed. The knots in the stalk form two useful segments to grasp it by. My pocket knife strips away the fibre, caresses its belly, its breast, its back. I cut into the tip and split it so that it will retain the ink. With my elbows propped on the sheet of paper, I soak the stalk in the liquid, allowing my muscles to relax. I dip my *qalam* in again; the stalk drinks the ink and I drink the air. It sometimes happens that I would like to swap roles, but calligraphers know that ink has no need to breathe. The scratching of the reed does not frighten me. My movements are mirrored to infinity. I am economical with space – the base line is straight, in spite of the interlinked letters. The shapes loll and stretch inside me. I stop at each junction, then carry on with the line where it has dried, and rest the tip where it rose. The character I draw is black and opaque. I am deaf to the cries of the reed; only my pleasure counts. I suspend my movement when the tip wounds the paper. These regular pauses are so frustrating; I would like to be ink so as to keep my *qalam* permanently replenished, with my breath becoming blotting paper and my skin a film of glossy paper. The urge to write a letter puts an end to my fatigue.

My dear son,

Your letter made me very happy. My mother and my sister fought to read it. The postman sowed discord in the house. We can imagine the timbre of your voice and the air of concentration on your face as you wrote it. 'It's the handwriting of a scientist,' says Evliya, an expert graphologist. The vertical sweep of the consonants is a sign of ambition, the width of your margins reveals great generosity of spirit.

This letter no longer holds any mysteries from us, except as regards its author. When you left, you were just a small boy.

I had some news of you from my Aunt Myriam, who used to go and see you at boarding school when she was staying in Beirut. She took a photo of you each time, and the photos were carefully arranged in my bedroom. Each time she got back to Aleppo, she wrote long letters to me, describing you in every last detail. Do you remember the photo taken at the door to the refectory? It sits enthroned on a pedestal table with a lock of your hair, cut by Hateme on your fourth birthday.

Even though Rashida is eighty-six years old, she hasn't forgotten your first steps; she had found you on the wooden landing stage, just about to jump into the Bosphorus, though she had left you on a chair next to the linen basket.

Do you remember our yali? *You used to call it 'the big tortoise'…*

Nedim is really looking forward to seeing his little brother again.

We hope to see you soon.

With big hugs.

Your mother,

– Rikkat

Nour's letters are all filed away in a folder that I keep close by. I often reread them. This correspondence has transformed my work. Now I dare to indulge in strange compositions and transgress the reign of the line, refusing to submit to the decoration. Saturated by my pupils' exercises and having to mark their exams, I amuse myself by mixing up the letters and superimposing their bones. I stick daggers into their limbs, so that trails of blood stain the paper. Sometimes the line gets tired, allows itself to be drawn out like a thread stretched to breaking point. At other times, disorder strikes me as quite harmonious, and the torture of the sign seems more agreeable to the eye.

Reading Nour gives me the strength to go on, to invent.

If a letter is late arriving, if a month goes by without me receiving any news, I relapse into banality. My hand made a confession to me a few days ago. It prefers my wild eccentricities to traditional compositions and encourages me to continue along this path.

Muhsin is more sceptical. He does not know which way to read my compositions and stares in wide-eyed astonishment at the sight of a truncated letter or a line that tapers away. He says my colours are disquieting; they come from Hell.

I can no longer work the way I used to; my flowers have a smell of rotting and my golden illuminations bleed persistently. The world has changed and gestures have replaced words. Mushin warns me: the Academy of Fine Arts spurns all innovations. They extol the aesthetic dimension; you prefer realism and liberty, he tells me. The work is immortal when the gestures behind it are invisible.

Paris, November 1957

Dear Mother,
I'm sorry, but I don't think I'm going to be able to come and see you. Here I am, settled into a little flat on the rue de

Solférino. Life in Paris is dear and I don't have enough money to travel that far. Father has stayed in Lebanon, his job comes to an end next year. The Seine flows a hundred metres away from me and I often go out for a walk along the quays at nightfall. My department is less than a mile from my block, it's a very fine building in dressed stone, and some great scientists have their names engraved on the façade. I'm looking forward to starting my studies...

Why don't you come and see me here? My room is big enough for two. The Louvre is just over the bridge. You could see the collection of Ottoman objects. There are so many places to visit; I'd like to discover these wonderful things with you.

Lots of love,

– Nour

Beylerbey, November 1957

Dear son,

I've been invited to Lisbon next February to restore some miniatures that belong to the Gulbenkian Foundation; I could stop off in Paris on my way back and see you. The secretary of the Foundation has requested help from the Academy of Fine Arts in Istanbul to restore a page of a manuscript that dates back to the fifteenth century. This is the love story Layla and Majnun, *comparable to the tale of* Romeo and Juliet *in the West. The way it's set out on the page, the colours and the decoration are typical of the school of Shiraz. My hands are longing to tidy up the margins, remount the backing and liven up the colours.*

The idea of getting to know Paris in your company fills me with delight. I am keen to discover the poems of the famous Bâkî in honour of Suleiman the Magnificent conserved at the

Bibliothèque nationale, and the drawings of the great Sah Kulu. Paris has so much for my eyes to gaze on. Have you already seen the letter addressed by Suleiman the Magnificent to François I? It's supposed to be difficult to see it personally... The Academy of Istanbul is going to try and obtain special permission for me.

I'll go to the railway station in Istanbul tomorrow to get the details and I'll let you know.

Hoping to see you soon,

– Rikkat

Rashida and Hateme envy me. They would like to slip into my luggage and become mice to see him just for an instant. I've promised to bring some photos of Nour back for them – profile, full face and even from behind. Nedim has prepared a letter that he has forbidden me to open. Rashida says that he slipped into it a photo of the most beautiful girl in Beylerbey. He would like to see Nour married to a local girl. Turkish women stay virgins until they marry.

My train tickets are on my bedside table; I look at them each evening before I switch off the light. Will Nour recognise me after all these years? The old woman I have turned into does not look at all like the young woman he left behind. And will I recognise *him*? The only photo I received from him two months ago shows him in profile outside the Abbey of Sénanque. My Nour looks like any other visitor.

I crossed more than five countries to reach my destination. Lisbon seemed like the end of the world.

The members of the Gulbenkian Foundation were very welcoming and the Islamic works of art that they possessed far exceeded my expectations. As well as that, there was talk of organising an architectural competition to build a museum that would be worthy of housing these objects. The miniatures were showing signs of wear and tear. They were kept in metallic racks sheltered from the light. I thought of the artists who had painted these legends over five centuries ago. I could imagine them hunkering down, turbans on their heads, delicately laying in their colours. Their faces are round, their eyes almond-shaped, and a sparse black beard distinguishes them from women. Their equipment is worn down by the pigments, their hands eroded by having to grind the metallic oxides: cobalt blue, manganese yellow and the green obtained from chrome and copper. They smell of sweat and regularly shake out their shirts to give their damp armpits an airing. Young prepubescent boys change their water, clean the paintbrushes, mix the colours. When they are too naughty, the master tells them off; silence guarantees the perfection of the outline and the precise application of the colours. The producers of ceramics are in the room next door. The temperature is high; the stove situated in the yard outside the studio emits an acidic smoke. The glassy coating necessary to waterproof the hardened paste has a strong smell, attacking the eyes and the nostrils. The draughtsmen have a repertory of very varied shapes, in which you can find cupbearers, princes sitting on their thrones and fantastic animals. They work very hard.

Three miniatures were produced for Sultan Iskandar who reigned in Shiraz at the start of the fifteenth century. The one that has deteriorated the most represents Majnun weeping over the tomb of his beloved, Layla. The work has already been restored over twenty years ago. The repainting is visible in the corners. Majnun's face has been stained by a careless hand. Some touching-up of the paint is required, especially on the dead woman's sarcophagus. I take the page out of its mounting and on the reverse side I discover the owner's seal written in Persian. The words 'lot no. 13' indicate that it was acquired at a Paris auction.

I reinforce the pages that have been torn on the back, smooth over the folds that have made the layer of paint start to crack, and remount the sheet of paper on a new cardboard backing. My fingers bring the colours back to life, and the page reawakens from its long slumber, thanking me for the care I have lavished on it.

From another drawer, I take out a miniature that has remained intact over the centuries and analyse its execution. Prince Bahram Gur is entering a mysterious pavilion and discovering the portraits of seven princesses, with whom he falls in love. The architectural perspective and the proportions are imprecise, and the characters seem to be moving in an intangible space, and yet you cannot help but admire the craftsmanship. I do not touch it but slip it into a folder.

The last miniature is more anecdotal; it represents a well-known episode from the life of Sultan Iskandar. Hidden behind a rock, he is observing some sirens who are bathing naked in a lake. His head is sticking out and you can just see his malicious eyes and moustaches shaped like swallow's wings. I need to touch up the water of the lake, which was clear blue and has turned to a muddy brown, and remount the margins, which are giving way under the points where the glue has been applied. Freed by this pressure, the page curls in on itself. I insert it between two pieces of cardboard to flatten it.

I have backache. I do some bending and stretching exercises to relax my neck. I interrupt the exercise when I spot a strange object. A jade pitcher has caught my eye; I go over to it and read the label tied around the handle: 'Pitcher from Ulug Beg, Samarkand or China, 15th century'. The whiteness of the jade and its degree of polish are so amazing that it looks like silk paper. I caress its belly and try in vain to detect any roughness. I would have said it was a Chinese pitcher if there had not been inscriptions in Arabic around its neck.

'This pitcher belonged to Ulug Beg, the son of Tamerlane. He would pour all his drinks into it. Jade can detect when poison is present and breaks into a thousand pieces when it comes into contact with an even slightly dangerous body.'

I turn round. The curator has come to pay me a visit. Pedro Bento knows the historical record of all the objects in the Foundation off by heart. The pitcher from Ulug Beg is his favourite.

We take a fascinating stroll through the basement of the building and Pedro is the ideal guide, able to explain the provenance and date of every piece in this collection, which comes from the four corners of the world.

His descriptions are interspersed with references to religious iconography. Old altarpieces or religious pictures are crammed with Catholic symbols. I find it hard to take my eyes off an Annunciation painted by a Flemish painter; Pedro reveals the symbols hidden in it. The Angel Gabriel is announcing to Mary that she will bear the Son of God. The dove hovering over their heads represents the Holy Spirit and the structure of the window conceals a cross. The garden in the very depths of the painting symbolises the Heavenly Paradise. I stand transfixed in front of this panel. It is impossible to move away. The Angel Gabriel sets me thinking of the dead calligraphers and especially Selim who bequeathed his skill to me.

'Did Mary love Joseph?' My question embarrasses Pedro. What answer should one give to a Muslim woman fascinated by a Christian work?

'She especially loved the son whom she bore from her union with God.'

I will not be using my instruments in Paris. I have cleaned them and rubbed them without managing to restore them to their usual gleam. A hazy film has covered the inkpot and my scissors have come unscrewed. And I just can't find that wretched screw! My tablet is in very poor shape, as if it had been used by a hundred other calligraphers. My hands have grown old too, I have grown old... My equipment is suffering from its exile; it is no longer rocked by the waters of the Bosphorus. I have stowed it away in my suitcase. I will not take it out of its container again unless Nour asks me to. My week in Paris is going to be very energetic; Nour will go with me round all the historic monuments and great chateaus of the Paris region: Fontainebleau, Versailles... In that way we will get used to one another.

The trip from Lisbon to Paris takes forever and the landscape rolling past makes me brood over my anxieties. I am afraid of the silence, the reproaches. The rail route went along the Atlantic Ocean, and the sight of all the blue gave me renewed confidence, but each time we stopped in a provincial station I relapsed into doubt. I arrive at the station; the doors of the compartment are a long time opening. Nour must be here.

I walk up and down the platform, this way and that: no Nour in sight. My legs are trembling from dragging my suitcase around. Exhausted, I sit on my luggage and scrutinise the crowd. A young man points to a bench; in his view it will be more comfortable than my improvised seat.

'Thank you, but I am waiting for my son. He should not be long.'

The young man does not persist. Ten yards or so further on, he turns round and utters my first name, somewhat incredulously.

We stay there frozen for several seconds. My son looks like any other Frenchman; only his eyes express his ancestry. He carries my suitcase. We walk towards the exit without really looking at each other. From time to time, he observes me out of the corner of his eye – is he disappointed by the way I look? His father's penchant for beautiful women has not prepared him for this. I am rather ordinary looking, tall and stiff, with a profile as sharp as if a knife had cut it; neither flirty nor fussy – it must be a change from oriental women. Intimidated by my smile, he lowers his eyes when my gaze lingers on him. Nour does not like effusiveness and I feel it is out of place after so many years of absence. We understand one another.

In the taxi that takes us to his flat in the rue de Solférino, I notice his hands, long and fine like mine. This vision warms my heart; those same hands, hardly a year old, had pulled my hair and torn off my long pearl necklace.

Nour is very keen to make sure I am comfortable. He empties out his chest of drawers and sets up a screen between our two beds. Embarrassed by so much promiscuity, he leaves me and goes out to buy tobacco.

His flat is filled with medical textbooks, books borrowed from the library and records strewn on the floor.

We tame each other by avoiding anything over-demonstrative. No physical contact; my eyes embrace him from afar, my ears drink in his words. Visiting museums gives us plenty of things to discuss, and we learn about one another without talking about ourselves.

One evening, with the help of the wine, he confides in me. 'Father has never told me anything about you. I think he's got a very bad memory of your marriage. Did you ever love one another?'

'It was an arranged marriage. Your father had found a woman and a country. The calligrapher was not a good enough wife in his eyes. He would have preferred me to cheat on him rather than spend hours on end in my studio writing sura after sura until I was exhausted.'

'Piety can isolate people. Father Moutran made sure our prayers were collective. Mine were sung, and yours written. The result is the same.'

'My God does not listen, but reads in the shape of arabesques. My hand orchestrates this song in the same way that Father Moutran did his choir.'

Nour acquiesces, amused.

'A better solution, especially for those who sing out of tune. They can always imagine writing to him.'

This dinner, with its copious libations, has freed us from our constraint. We walked home arm in arm, ready to remake the world. The motionless waters of the Seine seemed to me very dark compared with those of the Bosphorus. Nour asked me to write the name of the Prophet in a medallion for him. My son, born a Muslim, had never seen the name of Mohammed spelled out.

Before going to sleep, our mouths awry with weariness, we talk to each other across the screen, telling each other of the events that have left their mark on us. The darkness liberates us from our shyness, and old anecdotes make us laugh until we cry. These conversations become habitual. We go right to the end of the story, each one in turn, and it is forbidden to interrupt the one who has started. The screen set up between our two beds obliges me to speak loudly when I would really like to whisper.

I have described our *yali* to him, the gardener's shed, the fragrance of the rose-flavoured sherbet made by Hateme on days when it was really hot. 'When you were barely one year old, I hoisted you onto the window ledge so you could hear the song of the muezzin in the lower town. You stared at the sky, convinced that the voice was coming from the clouds, from a God who intervened at fixed hours. I pointed out to you the slender profile of a minaret so that you could make out where the song

74

came from. You held out your hand, waved your fingers as if to grasp the microscopic silhouette that was calling the faithful to prayer. You needed time, years perhaps, to realise that you were miles away from it. You put your dumpy little fist on my mouth as if to stop me singing when I tried to copy the modulations of his voice: *La ilaha ila Allah*.[43] Mehmet, a convinced agnostic, concluded that you were indeed your father's son. He did not believe in just one God, nor in just one woman.'

Evening after evening, Nour told me of the childhood he had spent far away from me. Father Moutran was his mother, Father Kamil his father. During the summer holidays, the latter would leave him for days on end in the schoolyard with a ball under his arm, which the boy would hurl furiously into the basket when solitude overwhelmed him. He lost his appetite, and was visibly growing thinner. Diagnosing a case of anaemia, Father Moutran made him swallow glasses of water into which he had dipped rusty scrap iron.

'Drink this, iron boosts your red blood cells.'

September brought his school friends back with the first rain. They were the brothers he did not have, the cousins of which he dreamed. He experienced their holidays, and uttered the words 'father' and 'mother' vicariously. His own father claimed to be overwhelmed by work. The anaemia went away as soon as he had the joy of company, and thanks in particular to the rich store of food hidden under the bed of his neighbour, who was spoiled by his family.

I go to sleep with his voice in my ears. He wishes me good night and turns on his side. His eyes stare at the white wall. Mine observe a crack in the ceiling, shown up by the light from a streetlamp. We both succumb to a deep sleep simultaneously.

The pattering of rain on the window of the flat puts me in mind of a painful incident. Nour was a newborn baby at the time. I had only just got over the birth, and had settled back into my studio, with my instruments and my blocks of paper. My hand started to rediscover the joys of calligraphy after a long period of inactivity. It was raining that day; the windowpanes of my studio shut me off from the rest of the world. Time sped by, my body quivered at the sight of the carefully traced rectangles ready for pious letters to be inscribed within them. Mehmet was fretting, wanted me to go out; he burst into the room, insulted me in Albanian, tore up the composition and then dragged me outside after slamming the door. He kept the key for a whole month in his jacket pocket. I could imagine the shreds of paper scattered on the ground, the dried inkpot, the ink turning to dust, my paintbrushes as stiff as the corpse of our cat as we had found it one winter's morning. In the spring, he opened up the room and was surprised to find everything in good order. The chair was back in its place, the instruments as neat and tidy as on the day of the incident. There was something stranger: the shreds of paper had been put back together without the least trace of glue. Someone had got into the studio and pieced together my composition. But who could have written this long text in such fine handwriting?

Whenever Ali, God's blessings be upon him, was asked to describe the Prophet, peace be upon him, he would say:

'He was neither tall nor short, but of medium height.

'His hair was not short; it was neither curly nor straight, but between the two.

'His face was neither narrow nor altogether round, but it had a certain roundness to it.

'His skin was clear, and his eyes black with long lashes.

'He was well-built, with broad shoulders.

'He had no hair on his body, apart from on his torso.

'He had big hands and big feet.

'Whenever he walked about, he would move with his torso bent forward as if he were going down a slope.

'When he looked at someone, he looked him straight in the eyes.'

I recognised the broad old-fashioned ligatures of Selim. It was some time since he had shown himself. I suspected that he did not much like my husband, whose Albanian manners must have put him off. My distress must have softened him. He had tidied, dusted, cleaned, then stuck together the scattered shreds of my composition, before vanishing. Being dead as he was, nobody had been able to distract him, and Selim had taken all the time he needed. The Prophet had finally welcomed him into his paradise, and he was leaving me the written proof. Only the blessed have the power to comfort and relieve human beings.

Nour's snores will not stop me from bringing the tale to an end. My ghost stories have made him slip into a deep sleep. When he is woken at dawn, he will tell himself that old Selim was merely a creation of his tired mind.

Now it is Nour's turn to speak. With his arms folded under his head, he narrates his story with his eyes fixed on the ceiling as if he were reading his past there.

He was fifteen years old and spent the summer between Beirut and Jounieh, a little coastal village, perfect if you wanted to embrace earth and sea in a single blink of the eye. He had followed his father, who was again taking an interest in him. Pierre had got to know a rich perfume merchant who lived in Saida, a Muslim fiefdom in the south of Lebanon. They spent the day visiting the monuments and wandering through the narrow alleys that led to the port. Nour was horrified by the carcasses of meat hanging from hooks, ready to be cut up by the butcher's knife. He felt violently sick, and went to vomit in the corner of a deserted street. An old woman, sitting on her doorstep, mopped his brow, gave him a drink, and pushed him towards a nearby mosque, where she forced him to kiss the Koran. Nour obeyed without knowing what he was doing. His father was supposed to be looking for him, but Nour cared nothing for this. Like an automaton, he advanced slowly towards a room that was bathed in half-light, where prostrate men were repeating in unison the *shahada*: *Allahu akbar, Allahu akbar*.[44] He gazed for a long time at the silhouette of the officiating imam standing against the pillar, then at the niche that was supposed to represent the Prophet, the mihrab, situated on the wall facing Mecca. He did not at all feel as if he were in a foreign country and had the impression that he had come back to his own people. These masculine voices were familiar, and the sight of their soles folded on the prayer carpets was part of a distant past. This conviction was soon forgotten when a hand pinched his ear, obliging him to get up and leave. His father did not let go until they were outside the complex. The old woman was no longer there to witness to his good faith, and Nour had no proof of his innocence. Once the incident was forgotten, he retained the echo of those voices punctuated by the plashing of the fountain for ablutions.

That evening, their host presented him with a medallion engraved in the name of the Prophet. Nour kept it preciously until the start of term, turning it into his secret fetish, which he slipped into a pediment behind the door of the confessional.

During the daily masses, his eyes would gaze in turn at the crucified man hanging aloft on the altar and then the medallion, and he was proud that he had brought the Messiah and the Prophet together in the same space and on the same level.

Nour must find my stories very strange compared to the minor transgressions of his youth. I would like to tell him a funny story, but nothing has made me laugh for a long time, apart from that story related by Mehmet during one of his visits to Istanbul. He wanted to impress us and kept bombarding us with historical facts that he considered 'of world importance', and in which he always assumed a key role. One example was the plot hatched against King Zog of Albania. Rashida, Hateme and I listened to him attentively. He said that Zog was a very controversial figure to his entourage, who criticised him for signing the Albanian–Italian mutual assistance treaty. They had chosen none other than Mehmet to kill the king. Armed with an old revolver, he waited for Zog on the steps of the parliament and, as was his habit, came out with a long speech, instead of blowing him away. Without a pause, he said, 'You must die, Zog, so that the Albanian people can survive.

'You have sullied the honour of our fatherland, sullied the blood that flows in our veins.

'You have sold the pride of your people cheap, by casting it into the arms of fascist Italy.

'You are an unworthy king.

'In the name of the Albanian people, I am killing you so that our people may finally free themselves from the harm you have inflicted on them.'

Disarmed by the guards who had rushed up, disowned by the organisers of the plot, he continued to harangue the King even when he was handcuffed. Poor Mehmet, he thought his exploit would dazzle us, but we laughed until we cried.

That evening, we realised that he had been pardoned by the King, but would never again be permitted to set foot in Albania – which was why he had settled down for good in Turkey and come to live with us in Beylerbey.

Nour is telling me about his arrival in Beirut in 1945. He was six years old. He was admitted into the first form, and was baptised at dawn. Total immersion for the son, while the father merely grazed the water of the font with his forehead. An over-hasty sacrament, performed by an ill-tempered Father Moutran. He distrusted the Albanian who changed religions the same way that other people change shirts. Nour made his entrance into the class with a wet head, coated with holy oil.

His classmates avoided him. He played by himself, his marbles clutched to his chest, friendless, without the least sweetie for a treat. He cried when the dormitory was plunged into darkness and had to struggle not to wee in the bed. His father came to see his son the first three days, then once every three weeks, then once every three months. Years went by. Pierre put on an act of religiosity, visiting monastery after monastery as well as the sanctuaries of Saint Charbel and Saint Rita. Sometimes the son would see him climbing the slope of a monastery dedicated to some celebrated saint, then falling to his knees and beating his breast until he drew blood.

Nour had to confess every week on Friday mornings, and he started the list of his sins with an act of contrition:

My God, I am heartily sorry for having offended Thee;
And I detest all my sins because they offend Thee, my God,
Who art all-good;
I firmly resolve, with the help of Thy grace to confess my
*   sins,*
To do penance and to amend my life.

I almost asked Nour why he spoke to God so informally, as 'Thou', but this question would have been a transgression of our ritual. Then it was my turn to speak. All my thoughts went back to that summer's day in 1945.

'Your chest was puffed out with pride, you were brandishing your cardboard suitcase, you took your father's hand, taking care to keep up with him. You darted a malicious smile at us when you crossed the porch that we normally forbad you to approach. Mehmet forgot to close it, and the wind added to our pain the noise of the wood slammed shut by the draught. Rashida and Hateme ran to close it, but I would have preferred it to slam a hundred times, a thousand times, all my life long, so as never to forget that day of misfortune.

'I did not cry, and went straight up to my studio, deaf to the appeals of my mother and my sister.

'I drew marvellous things that day; my hand never ceased to dazzle me with its skill. Of that self-reclusion, all that remains is the acid taste of ink in my mouth. Rashida and Hateme found me lying on the ground, with the dried-up inkpot next to me. I had swallowed its contents to the last drop without managing to kill myself. They thought I was poisoned, but I was simply dead drunk. In my semi-somnolent state I imagined arabesques of boundless splendour. I painted letters as fine and smooth as the hairs on your head. The parting in the middle separated them into two parts.

'So God did not want to take me on that occasion. He was in no hurry to welcome me. He will not allow us to depart this life without having presented him with one last work: the most beautiful, it appears.'

We were never the same again after this story. We had nothing left to say to each other; Nour and I were like two lovers who have devoured each other with such passion that they have freed themselves from their love. We had exhausted our resources, emptied our hearts and our memories.

I wanted to return to our family home, get back to our *yali*. All these night-time stories had wiped out my real life. I no longer had any past.

Nour promised to come to Istanbul before the end of the year; he wanted to see the notches I had dug into the doorframe of his bedroom to measure his height: up to three foot before he left for Lebanon. I often imagined the notches I might have made during his absence; Aunt Myriam should have written to give me details of how he was growing each year.

Here I am, back in my house and my studio. My mother has lost a lot of weight during my absence. Hateme is worried about her health. The old woman finds it difficult to move around. We get together in her bedroom so I can tell her about my trip. The photos of Nour are kissed and blessed by protective formulae. Ecstatic to see how he has grown, my mother forgets her sciatica and starts walking again.

I spent only a fortnight in Europe, and yet they welcome me as warmly as if I had been right round the world.

My son Nedim is worried about the state of the family fortunes. He tries to prepare me for the worst: a property developer has been advising him to knock down the *yali* and build a six-storey block of flats, with the upper two floors for our family. The land is valuable; we could live more comfortably.

It is a painful discussion. The house has put down roots in the clayey earth of the Bosphorus and the pomegranate tree has been presenting us with its fruit every summer for half a century. This building has seen the birth of a dozen babies and the death of five old men. It has heard the cries of pain of several mothers giving birth and the imperturbable silence of funeral wakes. It has accompanied the family in its happy and unhappy events without ever complaining, except perhaps at our negligence. It has accepted the floodwaters of the Bosphorus and the collapse of the cedar tree on its roof during the great storm of 1932.

Nedim is afraid that making sacrifices will not be enough to pay for all the repair work that this ruin requires; every month it needs the services of a plumber, a chimney sweep and a carpenter. I have to think it over before I reach a decision: whether to repair or to sell this edifice built at the end of the nineteenth century, when Sultan Abdülaziz[45] had entrusted his architect Serkis Balyan with the mission of constructing for him a summer residence on the Asian shore of the Bosphorus. The rich notables copied the idea, but transposed into wood the indecent displays of marble in the palace next door. My great-grandfather would have liked this place, to escape the summer heat. In time, it became our main residence.

There are a number of stories attached to it, especially the legend that lies behind its name, *Dolphinia*, in allusion to the dolphin that got stuck under the garage. Caught in the narrow basement space, it lashed out with its tail so violently that it made the walls shake. Awoken by the tinkling of the chandelier and the creaking of the walls, our great-grandfather thought it must be an earthquake, before he realised what was causing the din. He freed the dolphin by tying up the caique that was preventing it from escaping. On the day he died, he claimed he was going off to join the silvery dolphin, who was laughing with his mouth wide open. I have often imagined this scene; the animal's chirrups still echo in that unused garage. For over fifty years, the mosaic figure of a dolphin has adorned the entrance to the *yali*.

Nour will never again see the little house of his childhood, nor the garden shed. As for the path leading to the Bosphorus, it will be concreted over like the coast road to Büyükdere[46]. Our old hovel will crumble all at once, in a crash of dust, and the articulated arm of the mechanical shovel will take away the debris. It will not take long for it to see off this wooden corpse. The rubble will be reduced to a dirty little heap in which the boards of the parquet floor will lie next to broken windowpanes and torn curtains. Buried inside the creaking fortress, my studio will take with it the hours I have devoted to perfecting the work.

Nedim dreams of moving his family into a modern apartment with solid partition walls. He has asked the builder to provide him with exclusive access to the Bosphorus so that he can fish in peace and quiet. The truth of the matter is that he has had enough of playing the plumber and heating engineer and repairing the staircase.

He urges me, keeps singing the praises of life in an apartment, but his arguments come up against a single condition: I will not destroy anything until Nour has revisited the house of his childhood. He announced his imminent arrival in his latest letter; his trip will depend on his exam results.

In the same letter, he told me that his father had arrived in France. Nour has found him a new apartment in the residential outskirts of Paris, in Boulogne. His studies come first: his father would not have respected the rhythm of his work and the hours of revision he has to wrest from sleep. They meet up on a Sunday and have lunch in a brasserie.

One morning, after a night on duty at the hospital, Nour caught the woman from the Boulogne bakery in his father's bed. The great seducer had fallen back into his old habits; he still liked nice, plump women.

The old man can already see his son's plaque on the façade of a Paris block and his bowtie in place to reassure imaginary patients. Nour would prefer to do research, but he does not insist. The differences between father and son are great. The meagre income that the latter picks up from his sessions on night duty is pitiful compared to the extravagant expenses of the former: it's all swallowed up on 'crossed button' suits and starched shirts and sleeve buttons with their heightened 'cat's-eye' decorations, not to mention the 'little lunchtime snacks' in the elegant brasseries of Paris. Pierre, always careful to parade as many of the external signs of wealth as he can, mixes with Lebanese visitors and plays the role of the *grand seigneur*. After two years living beyond his means, his account is empty. And yet he continues to spend a whole month's budget in a single day; but since he cannot afford a taxi, the dandy contents himself with the metro to get home. His resolutions to spend less money last just two days, and his promises to behave better evaporate on contact with his desires: an alarm clock in burr walnut, a tortoiseshell fountain pen. These compulsive purchases force him to fall back on absurd justifications; he pretends that these ostentatious objects will be useful to Nour when he opens his doctor's surgery. 'Rich people feel at home with this kind of ornament, and you'll thank me one day,' he says, and yet there is no glimmer of gratitude on his son's face; he is tired of having to pay off his father's overdrafts and pacify the irate banker. On several occasions, Nour has to return purchases and get the money back. The Italian tailor on the corner of the Place Vendôme swears that he will never receive this insolvent customer again; his cheques always bounce, in spite of the gold pen that he unscrews with such panache. Pierre limits his peregrinations through Paris to limit these temptations, and yet he continues to choose his morning suit with the greatest care, matches his socks and his tie, sprays himself with scent and sits down in the salon armchair as if he were awaiting some distinguished visitor.

Boulogne is really rather dull in his view, and he would have preferred to share a nice middle-class apartment with his son in the rue de Solférino, where Nour has opened a pathology lab to supplement his income. The waiting room is in reality his bedroom and the fridge is filled with blood samples, cover glasses for his microscopes, and test tubes full of various secretions.

My son,

For two years I have been fondly nursing the illusion that I would see you in Beylerbey, but the summers go by and the turquoise waters of the Bosphorus never bring you to me. The house is going to be knocked down next spring; luckily we have a neighbour who will be more than glad to put us up during the demolition. Do you remember him? He built you a shed at the bottom of the garden. The new block will be finished in eight months. Your brother Nedim will live on the fifth floor, Hateme and I on the sixth. My mother turned eighty-two last month. She says she won't see the block finished. She wants to die before the scaffolding is taken down. My younger sister is upset when she thinks of the yali, *the last vestige of a vanished fortune and a prestigious past.*

I just let them get on with it. Life in the apartment may well be difficult, and I'll teach my pupils at home while waiting for the new university to be built.

Maybe you're right to give up the idea of coming back to Beylerbey, since too many painful memories cling to the house. Even when it's been demolished, it will still crunch under our footsteps. But concrete won't have the last word, the old foundations are too deeply rooted in the muddy soil of the Asian shore. Our bones turn to dust faster than the wood of its pillars. Don't forget to send me your news.

– Rikkat

Nour's reply brings a wind of madness sweeping down on the house. The glasses and the windowpanes tremble at Hateme's cries of joy, and our mother rushes over to seize the letter, forgetting her fragile bones. I read it out aloud, but they want to scrutinise every word with their own eyes. At the end of December, Nour will take a week off to come and see us.

Nedim takes pains to make his brother's stay comfortable, and has put a bed and desk in his room and made sure the caique is in good shape for their fishing expeditions. My sister and mother polish the room every day. The house has never looked so lovely. I am giving all my classes at once so as to finish the year's curriculum before he arrives.

The transfer of my course to the university disappointed my pupils. Calligraphy at home was like a meeting of initiates, akin to a secret gathering. The university has only just been built and does not seem the right place for this ancestral teaching that is delivered in an atmosphere of contemplation. The brand-new equipment produces sounds that are barely perceptible: the metallic pens groan on the whetstone, the tablets sag and the tracing paper gives way under the pressure of the needle as it picks out some famous illumination. There is total silence, apart from the breathing of my pupils, which comes and goes in time with their hands. They do not use all the air in their lungs, nor all the ink on their pens. I can already distinguish the talented pupils from the ones who will only ever be mediocre. Those who struggle on experience their art as suffering; they will never be true calligraphers. On the other hand, the most gifted are overwhelmed by a sense of plenitude, their bodies meld into that trail of ink that extends ever longer as their pleasure increases. They are outside time, outside themselves. Muhsin told me that writing was the calligrapher's sole carnal pleasure; that second of well-being, just as you hold in your breath to execute the gesture, is a much more intense experience than a shared orgasm. Our bodies enter into communication with the divine, perhaps even with death itself.

I can recognise the most gifted without seeing their compositions: their beautiful handwriting illumines their features, brings a bloom to their faces, and intensifies their gaze.

A good calligrapher emerges from this adventure looking haggard, and crosses the Bosphorus with eyes gazing sightlessly into the distance. He or she needs several hours to come back to reality.

Only Mehmet's hammerings on the door brought *me* back to reality. My husband was amazed to see me spending so much time doing so little. My travels were much too rich for me to reply to his attacks. Obsessed by my uninterrupted work, I would imagine the next stage while I did the ironing. Mehmet liked to read on my face the torture of unfinished work. How many times did I contemplate the stairwell of my studio and the narrow steps leading to it? I would turn away.

Mehmet started to go out more and more at night, and rarely saw his son. Nour would pull a face when the effluvia of tobacco and alcohol reached his nostrils. His father frequented the *gazino*[47] and would spend entire hours on the quays of Dolmabahce[48] before returning to the Asian shore. He had the glazed eyes of a drunkard and his breath stank: so the dolmus drivers[49] would refuse to take him, and he sometimes found himself on board a little fishing boat sitting on a wooden plank next to the fishing nets. The trip could last a good two hours, just time for him to sleep off his wine. I hoped he would forget our address. But he always came back to slip in between my starched sheets and succumb to sleep. He slept until nightfall. His sleepless nights ensured our days were peaceful. My mother would wake up, images of crime running through her mind, while I inhaled the acid vapours of his breath. I hated him in silence, right up until the day I could no longer remain silent.

Rashida and Hateme wept when Nour crossed the threshold. Nedim took him in his arms, in a long fraternal embrace, then carried his luggage into his bedroom.

The icy wind guided us to the chimney piece.

We gaze at the flames, happy for the sparks to break the silence. Nedim's chatter puts us at our ease, his wife and two children come to join the circle, and in the evening we forget our constraint. Hateme drinks in Nour's words and Rashida keeps rubbing his back, so as to reassure herself that he is actually here. We ate, drank and laughed until dawn. We women of the household went to sleep with a smile on our lips.

We strolled round the town, passed the doors of all the mosques, and wandered between the stalls of the covered market without a word of complaint. Nour's enthusiasm took our minds off our fatigue.

He listens to my tour-guide explanations and acquiesces when an explanation satisfies him. He is thirsty to learn, scrutinises the least object placed in the shop windows and tries to guess what materials it has been made from. Rashida waits for us at home, looking forward to our return.

Nour enjoys his food; Nedim and he can swallow a restaurant's entire menu and still have room for more. He wants to taste everything, compare everything. Rashida utters a blessing every time he opens his mouth. Hateme had to ask her to shut up. Nedim wants to take him to Büyükada,[50] where – he says – the best fish restaurant in the region is.

Nour is already well acquainted with every corner in the house. He enjoyed finding the doorframe with the notches indicating his height as a child. He has dug in a line to show how tall he is now. The gap between the last measure and the one he has just added is a big one, and the years that have gone by seem to me to be an eternity. He has even found the olive stone that he had stuck into the small latch of the door, now all shrivelled and ready to turn to dust as soon as a finger touches it. But Nour prefers to leave it there, pursuing a solitary existence.

My son's hands caressed the alabaster dervishes, and I re-minded him that when he was a child he broke the *seyh*[51]. He laughed and took in the palm of his hand the dervish who is dropping his mantle in sign of his renunciation of the material world. Nour likes to turn them over in his hands and allow the light to shine through the transparent gypsum. With a scientist's gaze he probes the material.

This morning, Nedim shook him awake. The sound of his rubber boots creaked on the old parquet floor. Nour swallowed a cup of coffee in one gulp and got dressed like a sleepwalker. He followed him onto the landing stage without a word as far as the caique that was moored by a wet rope. They said nothing, aware that a single word would have put the aquatic fauna on the alert. Nedim had prepared the fishing rods and the bait; Nour watched his brother's gestures attentively and repro-duced them with care. They rowed away: the same arm move-ments, the same cadence; then they stopped. From my window I could see only their bent backs, the caps on their heads and their breath that left clouds of vapour in the air. The Bosphorus was all theirs.

They whispered together, a long discussion that only the quiver of the nylon line could interrupt. The noise of the fishing rods' rotation made all sorts of fish come up to the surface.

A good three hours' worth of fishing. On the way home, Nedim took his brother by the shoulder and they strode along. Something had been troubling Nour, who could not manage to disguise his distress. They seemed to be very upset in spite of the bucket that was filled to overflowing. I immediately realised what the matter was: Nedim had revealed the secret that we had put away in a forgotten region of our memories.

What words did he use to describe the rupture? Never mind: Nour has to understand the reasons why his parents separated. He cannot go on living a lie, and neither his father nor his mother would have been able to tell him. The shame was too great and words sometimes derisory. I thanked Nedim for doing it in my place.

His stay continued in a cheerful frame of mind. Nour sometimes had moments of absent-mindedness, when his eyes stared into space. He must have been imagining the circumstances of the drama. I sometimes visualised that moment so as to prompt his imagination with the scenes that had left their mark on me. Nedim read his thoughts and nudged him to bring him back to reality. Nour treated Hateme even more nicely. She had not lost the grace that characterised her. She had preserved the same finesse and the same whiteness of skin. My sister was the most beautiful woman in the family and yet she had declined every offer of marriage: industrialists, bankers, merchants. I now remember with terror the way Mehmet stared at her, dazzled by her beauty, at our father's funeral. She had taken refuge in her mother's arms, intimidated by this stranger.

Mehmet's first friendly visits in fact concealed a love that Hateme rejected. Mehmet's one and only Turkish friend had seen through these feelings and warned him.

The monthly visits became weekly, and his eyes no longer stared at the gracious silhouette of Hateme, but at my sad gaze. Later on, he grasped my hand as I was showing him the pictorial differences between the decorative repertoire of the ceramics of Iznik and the more naive style of Kütahya; then he kissed me when I left him in front of the porch.

When he vanished, I produced some virtuoso compositions and wiped away the disquiet he had sown within me. My right hand, still quivering from his kisses, extended the inscription with vigorous gestures.

'God will not look at these last pieces of calligraphy. They breathe the pleasure and moist heat of your bed after he has passed by. Your suras have the acid smell of your sweat after your exertions. Calligraphers cannot enjoy satisfaction without the embrace of a *qalam*,' Selim whispered in my ear, indignant at the sight of his equipment being steered along by 'abject' thoughts.

Tired of listening to his sermons, I abandoned my studio. He insulted me, calling me – depending on his mood – a feather-brained sinner or an impious whore.

'Calligraphers do not have hearts to love with, but *qalams* to write with,' he kept telling me in his inaudible voice.

Nour left this morning. He said his farewells to the *yali* and hugged each of us to his breast in turn. I slipped a letter into his travel bag, asking him to read it in the train.

This departure was like the farewell in his childhood. The vegetation in the avenue was the same, sparse and in places burnt. Nedim embraced him tightly as Mehmet had done twenty years earlier. I felt as if I were sliding into an abyss; the same events were being repeated.

Nour unsealed the envelope when the train blew its whistle. Did my letter make him smile?

Beylerbey, 4th January 1960

My Nour,

I get mixed up with all your names. 'Jean' is too Christian for me; in Turkey, you will always be called 'Nour'.

You have restored our taste for happiness; what does it matter if the yali *is destroyed? That's really not important to us. The apartment block that will grow on that spot will be just as welcoming and it won't prevent Nedim from waking you at dawn to go fishing.*

You are the brother that he was deprived of throughout his early years; don't be cross with him for revealing our secret, you must share with us our happy and our unhappy times.

Now it is my turn to tell you the truth.

You were born just before the war, and it is often said that children who arrive during a conflict will not have united parents. Our country was not fighting the enemy, but war was present in everyone's mind. Your father and I very soon started to quarrel, and he started drinking. I shut myself away alone in my studio, to forget. He could not stand my indifference. The more serenity I found in my calligraphy, the more full of hatred he became. I would take revenge in my silence, and did nothing to appease his angers. Rashida, Hateme and Nedim endured this daily spectacle without a word, but my mother would take you out for a walk in the garden when your father's insults made the walls shake.

One morning, the house was awoken by the shouts of Rahmi, a fisherman from Beylerbey. His cries made his caique totter. My mother and I ran barefoot to the harbour wall; the drowning woman he had fished out of the icy waters of the Bosphorus was none other than my younger sister. We carried her back to the house; a thin trail of water followed our steps. Thank God, her heart was still beating. We dried her and warmed her up. The sound of our sobbing revived her. She was angry with us for having stopped her dying. 'What gave you any right, what gave you any right to do that?' she kept saying. The doctor who arrived a few minutes later reassured us as to her health, but the baby, he said, had not survived. 'What baby?' cried my mother, beside herself. She could have killed her daughter for real. 'Who is the father?' How could we keep the scandal quiet when the whole of Beylerbey was crammed into our front hall, trying to understand why the daughter of the great Nessib bey had been driven to try and put an end to it all? It was the next day, pressed by our questions, feeling harassed, that Hateme finally and reluctantly uttered the name of your father.

That same evening his suitcase was waiting for him on the landing. He hammered on the door with his fists, he was not going to go without his son. Then he walked resolutely to my studio, came in without knocking and grabbed the writing case, which he then flung through the windowpane; the Bosphorus swallowed it up.

That day, your father deprived me of my treasured possessions: you, and my old friend's writing case. Why did I let you leave with him? I thought I would get you back; I was convinced that that irresponsible father of yours would send you home.

He swept down the stairs and packed your case, piling in your clothes any old how. Rashida prepared a snack and you left with a smile. You know the rest better than I do.

Every day, Nedim would dive into the Bosphorus and search for the writing case. He never did find it. Curiously, in my mind it was linked to you; I needed at all costs to find it for you to come back to me.

– Rikkat

My mother died and was buried in the Eyyub cemetery in the family vault. I dictated her epitaph to the marble mason, who engraved the following:

Rashida Kunt, Usküdar 10th June 1882 –
Beylerbey 7th March 1960

We went back home and that night I dreamt of her; she was speaking to me distinctly and complaining about the thinness of the letters on her epitaph. She advised me to wrap them in warm coats so they would be able to face the coming winter. When I awoke, I asked the engraver to thicken the characters on her stele.

My life is no longer the same; Hateme and I live at the neighbour's, our house has been cleared away and the concrete foundations can be seen from the shore. Nedim and his little family are lodging with a cousin in the Sultan Ahmet district.

Istanbul has changed a lot, and so has our family. Even my works breathe the atmosphere of this prevailing modernity. Aesthetic conventions have been eliminated in favour of more natural and instantaneous motifs. My stylised rosettes or palms have been replaced by touches of bright colour heightening the outline of the letters. My words move about freely and wander across the paper, sometimes outside the frames that are supposed to contain them. My hand will not be tamed, and becomes wrathful when I try to discipline it.

'Construction and destruction' seem to be the keywords of our cycle. The concrete apartment block has grown quickly and has already found buyers. Hateme and I were the first to move in. We are on the top floor, with a view out over the Bosphorus that makes your head spin; I sometimes catch myself holding onto the walls, or hugging them as I go by when I start to feel giddy. My hand no longer works as it used to, now that we live high up; it skims over the paper and scatters ink as if it were a projectile. The filled-in spaces have swapped places with the blank areas, now that I am a neighbour of the sky. From my window I can no longer see terra firma, but that turquoise inlet of the sea that embraces immensity. My fingers beat their wings since they cannot move. They do not add up to much, when you think about it: a funny five-branched star writing atop an apartment block and closely observing the comings and goings in the strait. And yet these little hands are enough to cause a stir in the waters of the Bosphorus. When I am putting the finishing touches to a letter, a whirlpool comes into being; when my hand gets carried away, foam sprays the quays and then withdraws with the same intensity. I sometimes amuse myself by upsetting the tranquil course of this flow; I make the caiques pitch as they drop their fishing nets into the depths, or I make the boats sail against the early morning tide. But my hand is powerless against the liners that sail up and down the strait in a menacing silence; it drifts across the paper so that they can make their way between the frail vessels. By breathing on the ink to dry it, I drive away the thick fog of morning that blinds the travellers.

I press the metallic pen of my *qalam* and then relax my grip, depending on my mood; my hand alone decides the day's fate.

Hatame knows that the least disturbance could unleash a cataclysm. She waits for me to get up before serving me breakfast.

I give my classes twice a week at the university. After crossing the Bosphorus, I sometimes wander through the commercial districts of the city. I have few pupils, but they listen to me attentively. Calligraphy does not attract many students, they prefer to go in for more up-to-date subjects: modern art, architecture, sculpture... I have tried to explain to the school head that calligraphy is linked to other artistic forms, that the mosques of our country are overflowing with calligraphic friezes or religious objects that are inscribed with religious invocations. He told me that this discipline was too tied up with the Ottoman Empire and could not survive in our contemporary world. Ever since images have been permitted, beautiful writing has no further need to exist. Images are now omnipresent in our lives, but nothing will replace the elegance of inscriptions.

And yet, calligraphy can translate the sensibility of a new era; it is not frozen in time and must continue to evolve. The line of calligraphers goes on forever and ought to continue to the end of time. They alone are able to establish a dialogue between God and human beings.

Paris, 5th August 1970

Dear Mother,
Father passed away two weeks ago at the Garches hospital.
He succumbed to a stroke; he didn't suffer. He was buried in
the cemetery of the Raymond-Poincaré hospital without a
priest and without any friends. I neither wept for him nor do
I miss him.

What a strange character! A specialist in lies and sleeve
buttons, I said to myself when I saw his coffin being lowered
slowly and haltingly on its rope. Even his epitaph lies:

Pierre Ghata, Tirana 1897 – Garches 1970

He was born Mehmet Fahreddin Djaghataï to an aristocratic
Albanian family, got married in Beylerbey under the name
Mehmet Ghataï and died with the same forename as the first
pope. There were two of us at his funeral, myself and Mme
Tesson, the woman from the baker's in Boulogne, who wept
copious fond tears over him. It was she who dressed his
corpse, chose his tie and his best pair of shoes. He went off
in a made-to-measure suit from an Italian tailor's – the one
we all know about, on the Place Vendôme... It had cost me
an arm and a leg. I'd had to pay his bill in exchange for a
bouncing cheque.

Which God will greet him up there? His own religion was
women and money.

I emptied his apartment and went through his drawers.
I came across some notes he had written, a sort of collection
of fierce, ironic maxims:

Lie: something well dressed.
Honesty: a question of price.
Child: rainbow amid the storms.

Life: a disappointing excursion, the same for everyone.

I found albums of hand-coloured erotic postcards. Tits, pubes, lips and navels in pastel shades – these were firmer in outline. Circles and triangles were drawn in with darker pencils, and suspenders were completely reworked to suit his taste. And then I discovered this photo of Hateme posing for a photographer in the Beyoglu district. She is so beautiful, she must have been twenty. Nothing about you, no photos, no letters – it's as if you had never existed.

Well, there's nothing left of him except for his collection of suits that I have had shortened for me to wear.

I will soon be setting off for Lebanon to give a lecture. I haven't been there for thirteen years. Time goes by so quickly...

With big hugs,

– Nour

Nour had slipped the photo of Hateme into the envelope. I went to put it back in the album it had been taken from several years earlier. I announced the news to my sister. She turned her face away as if she had not heard, driving Mehmet out of her memories. My sister started to smile again; the death of her torturer had relieved her of that sense of dishonour. A shame that my mother is no longer in this world, she had been waiting so long for this event. As for me, my hand drifted for hours across the paper without writing anything; the movement alone was enough to calm me down. I wrote heaps of things with the help of my metal pen but without ever dipping it into ink. These transparent confessions were not meant to leave any trace behind them.

Old Selim read everything: the dead can read a blank; no syllable escapes from their lustreless eyes. Then he disappeared.

I pounded the paper with the metal point so that it would rain on the Bosphorus. Immediately, needles of rain started to fall on Beylerbey and I went to sleep to the sound of the deluge. For once, someone was weeping more than I was. I slept like a dead woman. The rain was unexpected (it was August), but as it fell, it wiped everything clean: my heart and my memory.

Ornamentation is my reason for living. My arabesques describe geometrical shapes, and I am the only one who knows their secret. Abstract designs: the stems stripped of their floral attributes turn into a line, and sometimes a point. God guides my hand, the composition acquires its own logic. The axes are multiple, but the geometry resists. The motifs echo one another in an interplay of darkness and light, reproducing the microcosm and the mysteries of creation.

My eyes close. The meanders swallow me up, the labyrinths bring me back to the surface. The zigzags, scrolls and spirals restore me to my life, to the happy and unhappy events in it. In the twinkling of an eye I recognise the path I have trodden; it is difficult to get away from these figures. Calligraphers are not free; escaping from this network of shapes is the same as disobeying the Most Great. Where are my lines taking me? My hand comes to a halt at the edge of the page; I will never know the rest.

The studio is bathed in darkness, and outside it is pitch black. The moon illumines my page as if telling me to carry on. I plunge into the darkness; the colours meld into one another. The patches of gold on the work surface gleam insistently. Following the trace of these sparkling fires, my eyes discover old Selim's phial. It is as full as the moon. Emptied, and kept as a souvenir of his ghost, it has filled up again after twenty years of oblivion.

The moon darts me a benevolent smile, the palms of my hands are turned towards it, as believers turn their hands towards the niche of the Prophet. I try to capture the dark star; the contours of the moon are reflected on my page, in invisible writing. I heighten it with gold to preserve some trace of it, and my hand follows the outlines of porous rocks. Old Selim's gold is too dazzling in comparison with the old sun. The writing is reduced to ashes; I can trace furrows in the fine powder, drawing endless arabesques; my page is as vast as the vault of the heavens.

Of that strange night nothing has remained. My mouth is dry, my hands eroded by the sand. All I remember is the scratching of the *qalam* on the sand's fine surface. An arid exercise; no ink has watered the thirst of the deep trenches.

Early in the morning, Hateme opened the windows, but an odour of sulphur hung in the room. Nothing to bear witness to the moon's visit: no composition, no golden ink, not even a grain of sand.

The phial that, the night before, had been full was now empty, the victim of a low tide. It will be refilled at the next sunset.

Waiting for the moon, night after night, takes away my desire for sleep. Sleeping has become a waste of time. My eyes have learned to guess at its hidden surface. We no longer have any secrets from each other.

Nour's letters are getting shorter and shorter, and his thoughts seem to be occupied by a woman. Calligraphers are never wrong; the jerky lines and the leaning characters are the signs of love. I have been waiting for whole months for him to admit it. He has been living with a woman for a year, and he wants to marry her.

I have not replied to this letter and pretend I never received it. I have related my sorrows to the tracing-paper, drawn a *bismillah*, then perforated the transparent paper with a metal needle to bring out its contours. The point wounded the paper and pierced my heart. I feel a mixture of pleasure and suffering. I took some time to realise that the needle was no longer holing the paper, but the skin of my forearm. Strangely enough, the blood respected the rounded contour of my arm. The tracing paper had become a receptacle for this thin line of red, and absorbed every drop. And then I stopped; the pain freed me, the mutilation was becoming too visible.

I replied to Nour. I wished him long years of happiness and a long succession of descendants. Nedim and Hateme offered him their congratulations in turn.

That day, I realised that only calligraphy had stayed faithful to me. Then I practised complex exercises and carried out some new experiments with collages and acrylic. My thick broad brushes left straight furrows behind them. I used my fingers as knives, and wood had replaced my paper. No more fine, virtuoso writing; my letters were becoming vigorous, multiple. My lines broke and shattered, arched their backs as my mood changed. I unwrote, pulverised the line and took control of the empty space. Broken, all the taboos of this science, and its rigid rules defied.

There were several of us who wanted to modernise calligraphy, but the religious labourers in the art of writing were afraid of drawing the lightning bolts of the Most High down on their heads. Those of us who dared to carry out these digressions were in a minority, and we were not at all worried by 'divine reprisals'.

I was frightened of nothing, and continued to offend him, each day a little more, dipping his praises in glue and covering them with newspaper. I hijacked all sorts of objects from daily use and introduced them into prayer.

As a result of infringing the rules, I have lost my faith. Now I fear neither God nor death.

As the years go by, my instruments push my hands away. I am getting on too much for them, too old to deserve them. I draw rooftops in charcoal, and the pressure of thumb reduces the carbon stick to dust. Everything disintegrates on contact with my fingers. Is this a warning? What is the explanation? Hateme made me a coffee; she turned over the cup and started to read the grounds. The sight of a funeral effigy lying in them seemed to terrify her. I pulled the cup off her, washed it in clean water and then dashed out to the landing stage; my pupils were waiting for me on the other side of the Bosphorus. I was just about to embark when shouts coming from one of our windows rooted me to the spot on the gangway. Hateme was waving to me to go back. The door was wide open, and my sister's voice as she spoke into the telephone was broken with sobs. She gazed at me, grief-stricken.

'It's your Nour, Rikkat – he died this morning. A heart attack while he was giving a lecture.'

I refused to believe her and grabbed the receiver off her. An anonymous voice from the other side of the world repeated the same words to me. What is going to become of his six-year-old daughter, I asked myself as my head spun – I was forgetting his wife, widowed so young.

In my studio I wanted to wall myself up alive. I did not give any classes that day, nor on the following days. Sitting on my chair, with my back to the light, I put my fingers in my ears so as not to hear the cries of Hateme who was begging me to open up to her. Outside, the autumn, the larch leaves fall with a dry rustle, the leaves covered with my writing ought to join them and disintegrate as they touch the ground. What am I supposed to do with these pieces of writing that will not give me back my son? What am I supposed to do with a God who uses my hand to write his breath? In any case, my fingers burn on contact with my instruments. They suddenly grew stiff and died at the same time as my son; all that remains is to bury them.

Exhausted from shouting, my sister finally forces the door open. Her breath sweeps across the back of my neck; she seizes my hand, slips a *qalam* between my fingers, and guides it across the page.

'Write, Rikkat, only writing will save you,' she orders me.

The trembling of my hand became evident for the first time when I was teaching my students, who noticed nothing. Everything skidded away under my fingers. The paper slipped, the *qalam* vibrated. Only my voice remained firm. Proud that she had been chosen from among my twenty pupils, Muna was illustrating what I had said, following my examples to the letter. I was incapable of shortening the loops, lengthening the upright strokes or correcting the proportions, and I suffered at the sight of the accents put in the wrong places. My hand gripped the table; I did not let go. Any excuse was good if it meant I did not have to set eyes on their work. The squat, truncated letters tortured me. I had put away my tablet and my cardboards, the silent witnesses of those short and increasingly longer tremors. Massaging my hands did not make the problem go away.

I decided to teach my pupils how to sharpen a *qalam*. My trembling vanished on contact with the reed; I caressed the stem with one hand and grasped the knife with the other. It had concave sides, and my thumb ensured it remained firm, but the slit wounded my index finger. Blood was spilled onto the stem. A last tremor made my right hand (the real guilty party) quiver.

Muna made me a bandage and washed the reed in clean water. The blood had given the *qalam* a strange colour.

There were twenty of them staring at me, observing my gestures. The knife kept that first drop of blood for a long time; it dried on the metal blade and in time turned black.

Once the class was over, I left the room, my hand gripping the handle of my bag.

Muna closed the door behind her after switching off the light.

I stood on the deck of the boat that shuttles between the two shores, my gaze fixed on Beylerbey. The outline of my village became hazier the closer I came. This sensation made me feel feverish. I was in a hurry to get inside its walls again, to forgive and to sleep.

My dreams, that night, swarmed with arabesques. Forms of writing that were difficult to discern dragged me into a labyrinth in which words and voices mingled. My body had become light; it was seized and drawn towards an opening; I went along with the flow and dived into a naked space. A sky as smooth as parchment, an ocean as opaque as ink, trees sharpened like *qalams*, the calligraphy instruments of the Most Great. My hand has pulled me out of sleep, it was now agitated by the same tremor as the night before. It reminded me of my terror when faced with the convulsions of my little Nedim. It is well known that when calligraphers' hands start to jerk, the end is near.

The whiteness of the walls calmed me. The steamed-up window of my bedroom filtered the first rays of the sun; there were rays that pierced the windowpane, while others were dimmed by the condensation. In spite of the fact that my eyesight had got much worse lately, I could read these lines without difficulty:

He is deferring them
To a stated term.
But when their term is come – surely God
Sees His servants.[52]

The writing faded away as I read it. Breathing on the windowpane and covering it with my breath did not help. This writing had come from I knew not where – were these lines a creation of my mind? Like a mirror, the pane reflected Selim's Koran opened at the same verse. God and Selim had finally joined together: perhaps they had never ceased to be one and the same person.

I died of asphyxiation, in spite of the efforts of Nedim who had transformed grandfather's hookah into an oxygen tube to spare me having to go to hospital.

Calligraphers die when they can no longer serve God.

Old Selim's writing case was miraculously found the day I died, shining through the waters of the Bosphorus. My son fished it out. It resumed its place on my desk a few hours after my burial.

I bequeathed my collection of calligraphies and my instruments to the Culture Ministry of the Republic of Turkey.

My funerary stele is richly sculpted; the epitaph, written by Muhsin, praises my piety and my talents as a calligrapher. He forgot to mention the rigour of my hand, its great perseverance when undertaking a task. When my hand wakes up, it sometimes complains about this omission. My compliments do not succeed in consoling it, and so it goes back to sleep, muttering incomprehensible words.

The pen falls from my hand. Dead as I am, what is the point of continuing to describe the void, the emptiness and silence. What will become of my work after me?

Epilogue

On 30th March 2000, in the Richelieu wing of the Louvre, Nour's daughter strolls through the rooms of the exhibition devoted to *Ottoman calligraphies: the collection of the Sakip Sabanci museum, University of Istanbul*. The writings break into fragments, the lines are interrupted by the translucent cases: flat panes of glass and protective windows reflect her face back to her. Her features are superimposed on the ink and the paper. Her reflection disturbs her: how can God be glimpsed if prayer reflects our own faces?

The curves get faster, slow down, the letters are infinite. The areas of flat colour are one-dimensional or deep. Too many voices and supplications...

Calligraphers renew their prayers, their overlapping voices express their thoughts in murmurs. Nour's daughter is unable to hear them distinctly.

Her gaze is drawn by an Ottoman poem. The golden interlacings of the outer margins are familiar to her. The exhibition label briefly describes the work and cites the name of a calligrapher: *Rikkat Kunt (1903–1986)*, her grandmother.

All she has kept of her grandmother is an ivory box decorated with golden foliage. Her mother used to tell her that she was a painter and that her paintbrushes had only two hairs, with at most a third one to colour birds' feathers. She has only one photo in which the old woman is holding her sitting on a table and smiling at the lens. Behind them, on the wall, two framed calligraphies have been hung on the wall, and the photo of her master Ismail Hakki Altunbezer in a hieratic pose.

All she has of her grandmother is a box, but the birds perched on its foliage wake her up at night with their twittering. Closing the cover is enough to silence them.

Bibliography

For the notes: the glossary of the catalogue to the exhibition *Ottoman calligraphies: the collection of the Sakip Sabanci museum,* 16th March – 29th May 2000, Musée du Louvre.

The Koran, translated by A.J. Arberry (Oxford World's Classics: Oxford University Press, 1983).

Calligraphers mentioned

Ahmed Karahisari (1470–1556)
Esma Ibret Hanim (b. 1780)
Abdullah Zühdi Efendi (d. 1879)
Ismail Hakki Altunbezer (1873–1946)
Necmeddin Okyay (1883–1976)
Rikkat Kunt (1903–86)
Muhsin Demironat (1907–83)

Author's notes

1. A pen made of reed.
2. A small plate on which the tip of a *qalam* is sharpened.
3. A portable writing case with an inkpot and a receptacle for *qalams*.
4. Timekeeper, responsible for the calendars that indicate the hours of prayer and the times when the fast can be broken during the month of Ramadan.
5. A story about the Prophet's words and deeds as transmitted by tradition.
6. The titles of suras.
7. A thin golden line framing the calligraphic text.
8. The imperial monogram of Ottoman sultans used to authenticate documents and other official pieces.
9. The letter M in Arabic.
10. A nickname given to Atatürk.
11. Better known by the name of Djalal al-Din Rumi, the thirteenth-century poet, mystic and sage, the author of the *Mesnevi*. The dervishes' lodge in Konya is the site of his tomb.
12. A Persian name that generally designates the spirits of evil and darkness. They frequently appear in Iranian epics, where certain of them assume a benevolent character.
13. In the Muslim conception, corporeal beings formed from a flame or a vapour, imperceptible to our senses and gifted with intelligence.
14. Paper scissors.
15. A university dedicated especially to teaching religious subjects.
16. A large-dimension calligraphic composition that can be framed and hung in mosques, offices and houses.
17. A formula put at the beginning of any important act on which one is calling down divine protection. It basically means 'In the name of God, the Merciful, the Compassionate'. This formula opens every sura in the Koran, apart from the ninth.
18. A reed flute.
19. Muslim dynasty (1077–1307).
20. The seventh day of creation as related in the Bible. The word 'Shabbat' means, in Hebrew, 'the cessation of all creative activity'.
21. Jewish festival celebrating recapture of the Temple of Jerusalem in the second century BC.
22. The pulpit from which sermons are preached in mosques.
23. Sura 68, verses 1–3. [Here and later (see note 52, below), I quote from the Oxford World's Classics translation by A.J. Arberry: *The Koran*, Oxford: Oxford University Press, 1983. – Tr.]
24. An Arabic recipe of the Middle Ages.

25. The palace of the Ottoman sultans built between 1463 and 1478 on the site of the old Byzantine acropolis.

26. Private apartments of the Palace of Topkapi.

27. Pious endowments (*wakf*): inalienable endowments of real estate or other donations used to ensure a charitable service or to build and maintain a religious or funeral institution.

28. Chancellery writing.

29. Month during which the Koran was revealed and month of fasting, described as 'venerated'.

30. Temporary favourite.

31. Old palace.

32. Round, hollow dish.

33. Pitcher with a handle.

34. Tankard.

35. Certificate of appointment carrying the monogram of a sultan.

36. Royal studio or workshop.

37. Name designating a decorative style inspired by Central Asia.

38. 'From Cathay: China'; floral decoration of Chinese inspiration, with lotuses and poppies arranged on simple whorls.

39. Long, slender leaves with jagged edges.

40. Motif composed of three circles and undulating lines called 'the Buddha's lips'.

41. From the word *gubar*, meaning 'dust' in Arabic.

42. Ski resort situated in the mountains of Lebanon.

43. There is no God but Allah.

44. Profession of faith.

45. Sultan Abdülaziz (1861–1876).

46. Village north of Istanbul situated on the edge of the Bosphorus.

47. Turkish nightclub.

48. Palace of the sultans built between 1843 and 1856.

49. Minibus or collective taxi that crosses the Bosphorus.

50. Island situated just off Istanbul in the Sea of Marmora.

51. Sheikh or master; as the focus of the ritual, he ensures the ceremony passes off in good order, murmurs instructions to the dervishes and moves round them.

52. Sura 35, verse 45.